"A panic attack of prose, slowly seizing your senses..."
—**CLAY MCLEOD CHAPMAN**, author of *Ghost Eaters*, *Vulture's* Best Horror '22

DEENA

UNDONE

DEBRA K. EVERY

DEENA UNDONE

DEBRA K. EVERY

woodhall press

Woodhall Press | Norwalk, CT

woodhall press

Woodhall Press, Norwalk, CT 06855
WoodhallPress.com
Copyright © 2024 Debra Every

Cover design: Asha Hossain
Layout artist: LJ Mucci

Library of Congress Cataloging-in-Publication Data available

ISBN 978-1-960456-13-7   (paper: alk paper)
ISBN 978-1-960456-14-4   (electronic)

First Edition
Distributed by Independent Publishers Group
(800) 888-4741

Printed in the United States of America

This is a work of fiction. Names, characters, business, events and incidents are the products of the author's imagination. Any resemblance to actual persons, living or dead, or actual events is purely coincidental.

To Aunt Mary

T.I.R.

PART ONE

1

Agatha stands at the edge of a lake staring at the water as she listens to the gentle waves lapping the shore. The ground is solid, the air thick with the peppery smell of a lone pine tree growing by the water's edge. A gentle breeze brushes across her lined face. She no longer needs the cane she has been using since her seventieth birthday. The arthritis is gone.

What strikes her is the strangeness of it all. She's still tethered to her hospital bed—feels the weight of her blanket, the hard pillow, the undercurrent of hospital white noise—all while standing alongside the water. She bends down and dips her cupped hands into the lake, bringing the water to her lips. It tastes sweet. Concentric circles gently ripple outward until they are absorbed by the water's surface.

Agatha realizes that the extraordinary vibrance of her surroundings is real. She can feel it, taste it, smell it. What's more, she senses a presence guiding her to a wellspring of darkness hidden below the surface. Clearly this is a way station of her own making. Why else would she feel a flush of warm anticipation?

She glances at her left hand with curiosity, wondering at the vibration in her fingertips. With a satisfying sense of release, she pulls off her fingers, one by one, and drops them into the lake, watching the blood turn the water black. As each finger sinks it expands, becoming a formless, irregular mass floating just below the surface. She gazes at them as a mother would her children, her need for a legacy finally satisfied. Naming them seems only right. *Visu. Auditu. Tactu. Gustu. Odoratu.* The embodiment of all that she is. Her five senses made manifest.

But something has been left undone.

Agatha turns away from the lake and prowls the barren landscape, searching. How wonderful to walk freely and without pain. In her wake, trees break through the hard earth, first as saplings, then as massive columns, celebrating her arrival. Leaves appear and unfurl like open palms. Soon she is surrounded by a towering forest, a carpet of moss and ferns under her feet. Seedlings beget shrubs beget bushes beget flowers. The citrus smell of lemongrass fills the air.

Agatha closes her eyes and summons an image of a woman from her memory. Not just any woman. *Her.* The woman carries a bundle in her arms as she makes her way around the edge of the newly formed forest. A spasm of resentment seizes Agatha as she watches her step onto a moss-covered path leading down to the lake. Agatha's eyes narrow into slits and a smile slowly spreads.

"Deeeena," she whispers. "There you are."

2

Deena Bartlett had been on the phone for more than twenty minutes, all while sitting next to her sleeping aunt at Wilshire Rehab Center. The stone ledge masquerading as a chair was every bit as uncomfortable as the one back at Hillcrest Hospital, where she'd spent the better part of a month watching Agatha descend into her final days on God's green earth. She could sense the accumulation of despair infused in the chair's fabric and frame from the hundreds, maybe thousands, of families who had been there before her, keeping watch over the dying. Maybe that was why she felt a growing unease. She was waiting for something to happen.

There had been a measure of hope during Agatha's stay at Hillcrest, even with her refusal of medication. That all changed last week when the seventy-eight-year-old was moved to Wilshire—her final stop on the road to Hallelujah.

Deena's current phone call wasn't going much better than the half-dozen before it. Nobody seemed interested in visiting her aunt. Not even Agatha's friend, Lucine, with her embarrassed refrain of *umms, ers,* and *wells*. Deena finally took pity on the woman and ended the call.

4

Lucine's reaction was surprising. True, Agatha hadn't seen her old friend in years, but the two women had known each other for decades. Loyalty ran deep in the Syrian community. Deena could only suppose that when it came to Agatha Haddad, loyalty wasn't enough. Her aunt was difficult, and as old age had collected onto her cantankerous bones she'd turned from bad to worse. One by one the people in her life vanished, leaving Agatha alone on a sinking ship with only Deena by her side.

When the call ended, Deena sat quietly staring at Agatha's four-foot-eleven-inch frame lying in bed like a nearly full sack of water threatening to undulate at the slightest touch. Her aunt's face was round and bloated from years of too much food and drink, her chin-length gray hair lank and lifeless.

There was no family resemblance between aunt and niece. At fifty-eight Deena was a handsome woman with a small frame and a mass of gray-streaked curls falling over the collar of her tailored shirt. She brushed a piece of lint from her pinstriped trousers, straightened the man's tie hanging loosely around her neck, and stared out the window . . . until a voice broke the quiet.

"How's it going?"

Deena turned toward the door where her husband, Simon, was leaning against the frame with his hand in his pocket and his right leg crossed over his left. After twenty-five years she still loved the look of him—tall and lean, with just enough awkwardness to keep him tethered to his younger self.

"Lost?" she asked with a smile.

"I had a break at school. Thought I'd poke my head in. Any change?"

"Nope. Still sleeping," said Deena. "I'm surprised to see you."

"I didn't come for Agatha. I came for you. But not without bearing gifts." Simon brought a white bag out from behind his back as he strolled into the room. "Ta-da!"

Deena's stomach gave a tug. "Big Belly's?"

"Nothin' but the best." He dropped the bag onto the overbed table, reached in, and pulled out a double-fist-sized bundle wrapped in butcher paper, along with two cans of Coke. When he unwrapped the butcher paper, the heart-stopping smell of pastrami filled the room.

"I even brought lentil soup for Agatha," he said. "That is, if she wakes up."

"You're a lifesaver." Deena hurried over to the table and grabbed one of the halves. She removed the top slice of caraway-studded rye, heaped a mound of coleslaw onto the pastrami, and then a healthy slathering of Russian dressing. For years she and Simon had argued about the perfect hot pastrami. Simon insisted that anything but spicy brown mustard was sacrilege. Not Deena. She liked her pastrami sloppy. Big Belly's may not have been Katz's from the Lower East Side, but it was damn good considering it was in Upstate New York.

Simon caught Deena eyeing him as he fastidiously spread mustard onto his half—edge to edge on the bread, never on the pastrami. Before she could denigrate his choice of condiment, he said, "Please, you're sullying my culinary experience."

She raised her eyebrows with her head pulled back as if to say, "Who, me?" and then focused her full attention on her sandwich, wiping drips of dressing off her hands and around her mouth. After not being hungry for days, Deena couldn't get it down fast enough.

With nothing left but the wrapper, she dragged her finger through an errant drop of dressing and popped it into her mouth. She then took a thirsty pull from her Coke, leaned back, and said, "I could use a shower."

Simon laughed. "Feeling better?"

"A bit."

He gathered up the empty wrappers, jammed them into the bag, and made a perfect trash basket three-pointer. With that done, he settled back into his chair and together they sat listening to Agatha's breathing, the only sound in the room. Lunch may have given Deena a welcome break from the day's heaviness, but it took less than five minutes for their extravaganza to be overtaken by the swirl of life's passing with a dying Agatha as guide.

Simon reached for Deena's hand and gave it a squeeze. But his smile quickly faded as he examined her face. "There's something going on. Spill."

Deena would have preferred not answering. Conversations about her aunt were dotted with land mines. It had always been best to avoid them. And in the spirit of *all-roads-lead-to-Agatha*, Deena lumped the rest of her family into the no-talk zone. But when a person sits day after day watching someone from their family die, the rules of the game change.

"I can't stop thinking about Mom," she finally said. "The way she took care of my grandmother."

"Understandable, considering where you're sitting."

"You should have seen the two of them. Mom never left that woman's side—all while Teta served up complaints like candy. I mean, this was her mother-in-law, for God's sake. Yet here I sit, with all manner of ungenerous thoughts rolling around in my head as I care for my own mother's sister."

"I suspect even your mother had her moments. It's easy to remember a person through a nostalgic lens."

"Oh, please," said Deena, shaking her head. "I was twenty-five when my parents died. I remember them both very clearly."

"You've got to give yourself a break. I may not have known your mother, but it seems to me that what you've done for Agatha is right out of her playbook."

"Maybe," she mumbled, turning toward her sleeping aunt.

Simon rubbed his face. "Deena, I'm worried. The past year has taken its toll. I'd hate to see you have a relapse."

And there it was. The first land mine. Simon's favorite axes to grind were Deena's mental health and Agatha, but combining the two into a creative ball of scrutiny was new. Agatha had nothing to do with Deena's years in therapy.

She stared at Simon with as steely an expression as she could muster.

"Okay," he said, with obvious disapproval. "A topic for another day."

"Look, once I get back to work, everything will be fine."

"I hope so. There are people who miss you. I saw Kayla Madden crying in the guidance counselor's office this morning."

Simon always knew which buttons to push. Deena felt a grab of conscience.

"Poor kid. I'll give her a call on Saturday."

"A call would be nice, but sessions with her acting coach would be better."

"We have all summer to focus on monologues. Her first audition isn't until November."

Simon narrowed his eyes, clearly waiting for more.

Deena added, "I'll figure something out."

"Good," he said, nodding. "So what do you think? Does she have a shot?"

"Juilliard or Tisch would be a stretch but, yeah, definitely . . . as long as her mother doesn't sabotage her. I think Kayla's got the goods for a bigger career than I ever had."

Simon checked the time on his watch and stood to leave. "I'd better get back. And I may be home late—it's my turn for study hall."

"Oooh. So my boyfriend can stay a little longer."

Simon laughed. "Have at it."

He reached her in two steps, bent down, and straightened her loosely knotted tie. Deena smiled up at him and delivered a good-bye kiss.

"Thanks for coming," she said. "It means a lot."

After Simon left she settled back into her book. Before long, Larisa Goodwyn's latest novel had grabbed her by the unmentionables as Deena waded knee-deep through the mayhem in *The Devil Beside*

Her. But the book's mounting tension was interrupted by a quiet "Help" coming from Agatha as she struggled awake.

The fact that her aunt had said even one word was surprising. For days she'd been in and out of consciousness, too weak to speak. It wasn't just the one-two punch of COPD and heart failure that was draining the life out of her. Sepsis had handed Agatha a front-row seat to *nevermore*, with her denial of medication acting as the coup de grâce. It was a surprising choice from such a selfish woman, but strength and control meant everything to her. Agatha would rather die than be sick. *Wish granted*, thought Deena.

She took her aunt's hand and said, "I'm here, Aunt Agatha. What do you need?"

"Help me up."

"I think maybe we should get your mind going first. Get you talking."

With that, Agatha smiled. Happy? Sarcastic? Hard to say. But her eyes struggled to become more present, more self-aware.

And then a switch turned on. Agatha's face regained its character-istic hard edge. With great clarity, enunciating each word so as not to be misunderstood, she said, "If all I need is to get my mind going, why the hell would I . . . need . . . you?"

Perfect, thought Deena. *Agatha Haddad. My family's contribution to universal kindness.*

As quickly as Agatha had delivered her words of appreciation, she dropped back off to sleep. Her aunt had always viewed whatever situation was at her disposal as an opportunity to score a criticism or denigration. Dying was clearly not cramping her style.

Deena leaned over the bed to fluff her aunt's pillow and give her sheet a tug. Then she got up from her chair and stretched the kink from her back. The days seemed to be getting longer and longer.

She walked over to the window and looked longingly outside, wishing she was in her living room laid out on the couch with a glass of wine. Deena combed her fingers through her hair and massaged the back of her neck, hoping this small relief would get her through another hour of sitting . . . when a woman's whisper floated into the room.

"Deeeenahhh."

Deena's shoulders flinched at the hushed sound of her name. She shot a look at Agatha but her aunt was still asleep—and there was no one else in the room.

Damn, she thought, shaking the whisper from her head. *Larisa Goodwyn knows her business.* Her new novel had clearly hit its mark. Then again, the whole morning had felt as if something was hanging in the air. It was time for a break.

With a just-in-case glance over her shoulder, she left for a cup of coffee. It was a relief to leave the confines of her aunt's room with its heart monitor counting off the seconds. If Agatha had been in her own bedroom surrounded by bits and pieces of a long life lived she may have felt a measure of comfort. But Deena knew in her heart that it wouldn't have made a difference. Her aunt's favorite pastime had always been finding creative ways to lash out.

On her way to the lounge, she passed Maggie Doherty's room to the left.

"There you are, Deena," Maggie called. "Come in and see me, you sweet thing."

They'd met a week ago. Maggie had been forging a path down the hall with her new walker when she'd spotted Deena standing at the nurses' station. Without breaking her stride Maggie had offered up a wide grin and said, "Care to dance?" It was a lifeline Deena couldn't help but grab. Over the next several days they'd spent a moment here and there, chatting together about this and that. Deena had felt an instant connection.

She put her coffee on hold and went into Maggie's room. The eighty-two-year-old was sitting up in bed with a book, surrounded by get well cards and flowers. Maggie was the quintessential Disney grandmother, petite and spry and funny—the type that baked cookies or knitted sweaters.

"How's it going?" said Deena, pulling up a chair.

"Better every day. Rehab is working its magic, yes, indeed."

"Looks like a concussion is no match for the unsinkable Maggie Doherty."

"I fell off a stepstool," she said, "not Kilimanjaro. So much fuss over so little. As I say to my children, 'Falling is God's way of saying wake up and smell the coffee.' "

"I suspect it's not the fall that's worrying them. It's the heart attack."

Maggie closed her book and gave Deena a mischievous smile. "Something's bound to get me sooner or later. At least I'll know what direction it's coming from." She patted Deena's hand and leaned forward. "Just remember, dearie, you can't live forever."

Deena laughed as she stood to leave. "I'm going for a cup of coffee. Can I bring you anything?"

"I think not, but you are lovely to offer. As I always say, 'Being nice is the rent you pay for your room on Earth.' Seems to me you're all paid up."

She is really something. Deena smiled broadly and left for her coffee. Maggie had shown up at just the right moment—as if her mother had stepped in to give Deena a helping hand while she sat, hour after hour, by her aunt's bedside.

When she got to the lounge, she helped herself to a cup of coffee and sat in a chair on the far side of the room ready to resume her current pastime: staring out the window. She was doing that a lot lately; staring out windows wishing she was someplace else.

After ten quiet minutes, she stood with a shrug, topped off her coffee, and reluctantly left. When she was a few feet from Agatha's room, she noticed a woman with a cleaning cart standing in the doorway, looking at her sleeping aunt. She was short and ample, with thick socks and sneakers, wearing a smock over a faded floral dress. The woman turned toward Deena at the sound of her approaching footsteps. When she did, the glare from the overhead fluorescent light cast her wrinkles into deep shadows and highlighted a slight drooping on the right side of her mouth.

She focused her milky eyes on Deena and motioned for her to come closer. When Deena was at arm's length, an arthritic hand darted out, grabbed her by the wrist, and pulled her in so close that a smell of decay coated Deena's throat. Was it her imagination, or did those milky eyes suddenly clear?

"Take care," whispered the woman in an accent she couldn't place. "She is coming for you."

Deena's chest tightened as the woman turned and wheeled her cart away, leaving Deena just a little stunned. *What the hell was that?*

Then, for the first time in years, her right hand began twitching. She quickly grabbed it with her left and stole a glance at the nurses' station, even though she knew nobody had noticed. The reflex was a holdover from darker days.

She turned into her aunt's room, fighting the urge to close the door. *Just a crazy old lady. Forget about it.*

But as the afternoon wore on, she found herself feeling the roughness of the old woman's hand with its swollen joints and gnarled fingers clamped onto her wrist like an ancient, twisted vine.

———

That night she had a dream.

She was walking along the edge of a lush forest, carrying a baby swathed in a blanket, frayed and threadbare. The air was filled with the fresh scent of citrus. Eventually she came to a moss-covered path flanked by ferns quivering in the light breeze.

Deena stepped onto the path and headed toward an ink-black lake in the distance. When she reached the shore she noticed five floating objects swirling lazily in the water, but try as she might, she couldn't make out what they were.

She leaned over for a closer look, and as she did a small hand from her bundle reached out. Deena looked down at the baby, but the hand was gone. The baby was gone. In its place was a rotting, maggot-infested piece of meat. The stench rose up into her face, watering her eyes and making her gag. Deena threw it into the water where the rotting meat transformed into a likeness of her mother.

"Deena!" her mother screamed. "Help me!"

Before Deena could get to her, the water—no longer water now—the thick, black, viscous liquid oozed into her mother's mouth and nose, with her mother's screams struggling to escape the mire. The oily bog took the last of her with a final, horrific groan as her mother's unblinking eyes slowly sank below the surface and out of sight.

Deena heard someone laughing behind her and, wheeling around, came face-to-face with her aunt holding a cigarette. Agatha dropped her jaw and a cascade of maggots flowed from her mouth while a voice in Deena's head whispered, *Ready or not . . . here I come.*

3

Deena fought her way to the surface, but the twisted images of Agatha, of her mother, of the black lake threatened to follow her into the room.

"Turn on the light!" she yelled.

Surely the light would save her. Surely it would keep the images at bay.

Simon reached for the lamp and flipped the switch. The sudden glare helped, but only just. He pulled her in close and whispered, "Shhh . . . I've got you."

It was three in the morning. She leaned against him, hoping the feel of his body would wrangle her heartbeat from a sprint to a quiet shuffle, but it wasn't doing the job. Deena brushed away the last threads of her nightmare and recited her dream to Simon in a river of words, a kind of exorcism, all while keeping her voice in a furtive whisper for fear she might rouse the demons crouching in shadows, waiting. When she was finished, she rested her head on his chest and listened to his heart until her own breathing finally slowed.

"This can't go on," said Simon. "You're exhausted."

"She's dying," snapped Deena. "What do you expect me to do?"

He started to answer, but then stopped as they lay together, too wired for sleep. Before long the sound of birds drifted through the window, and by 6:30 Simon was nuzzling his cheek against Deena's forehead.

"I want you to promise me something," he said, gently. "If you start feeling . . . I don't know . . . like you can't cope, promise you'll tell me."

Deena pushed him away. "For God's sake, stop. This isn't a make-or-break audition. I'm caring for the last member of my family. I'll be fine."

"High-stress auditions aren't the only things that can trigger a panic attack, and panic attacks aren't the only things that can derail a person. Your aunt has spent years chipping away at your self-worth. She does not get a free pass because of a few crumbs of attention flung at your feet when you were a teenager."

"Crumbs? I got my first off-Broadway show because of her."

"Okay, fine. But that doesn't give her the right to treat you like a doormat. What I don't understand is why you never pushed back. If anybody looks at you crosswise your impulse is to snap them in half. With all her harsh words and abuse, you sit in that rehab center for hours on end. Don't let her last days on Earth push you over the edge."

"Well, you needn't worry your pretty little head. Once my aunt is dead, your Agatha troubles will be over."

Simon took her comment like a slap. "That's not fair, Deena." He swung his legs around and headed into the bathroom.

Shit. Shouldn't have said that. Deena had given up trying to explain her relationship with Agatha. Simon came from the perfect Connecticut family where the gene pool had been cleansed of all harsh words and deeds. A well-played *Shut up* in the Bartlett clan would have had them running for the hills. But just because Simon couldn't understand why she hung in with Agatha was no excuse to lash out.

He finished his shower and was back in the bedroom pulling on a pair of sweats. She studied his face, checking for signs of lingering anger. With socks pulled up, sneakers tied, and eyes averted he said, "I'm going for a workout."

Yup. Still angry.

"Simon, wait."

He turned to look at her, his eyes unreadable, his mouth set in a straight line.

"I'm sorry," she said. "That was uncalled for."

"Don't worry about it."

"Can I have a kiss?"

Simon lowered his head and stared at the floor. It seemed he was about to leave, as his foot inched toward the hallway, but when he looked back at Deena his face softened. He walked to the bed, bent down, and kissed her.

"I'm not the enemy," he said. "You don't know how much I wish I could help with your aunt, but let's face it: The woman hates me. And you won't accept help from my sister *or* Fiona. She's your best friend, for God's sake. But I get it. You're the only one Agatha wants. All I'm saying is, you need to take care of yourself. Eat a decent meal. Get some sleep. Set aside some downtime."

Simon's face was so close that, for just a moment, the room receded and his eyes became the only thing in the world. Deena gave herself over, repeating the same silent promise she'd been making for years—that she wouldn't let her temper do the driving.

He brushed the hair from her forehead, pulled together a half-smile, and left.

———

Deena lay in bed staring at the ceiling for as long as she dared, but 8:30 still managed to bully its way in. Wilshire Rehab was waiting.

She threw aside the covers with a groan, got dressed, and ran downstairs. But when she grabbed the car keys from the vestibule table her eyes fell on a framed picture of Simon with a broad grin, holding an inviting glass of wine.

Maybe he's right. Nobody will arrest me if I get there after ten.

She pulled out her phone and called the nurses' station for an update. They said Agatha was fast asleep and stable. What harm would it do to take some time for herself? A cup of coffee. A bit of breakfast. Why not?

She did an about-face for the kitchen and found a recording of Mozart trios on Spotify—perfect egg-scrambling music. Fifteen minutes later Deena was sitting on the front porch with a plate of eggs on the table and a mug of coffee in her hand. It had been ages since she'd had a leisurely breakfast. Ignoring the guilt niggling in the back of her mind, she slathered butter on her toast and crunched down.

Deena never stopped being surprised at how much she loved living in the country. She'd always meant for Manhattan to be her home, and yet here she was, in a hundred-year-old house with old plumbing, drafty windows, and a symphony of creaking floors. But it was beautiful. The narrow winding road leading to their driveway was lined with old-growth maples. Whenever she drove up to the house she imagined pies sitting on gingham towels cooling in an open window while a border collie dug up bones in the front yard. Sure, winters were ridiculous. Their first power outage caught them with no supplies, no water, no nothing. But now, eleven years later, she couldn't picture living anywhere else. Rolling farmland. Miles of green. Perfect.

She sat on the porch nursing her coffee as she looked out over the garden. The sun sat above the surrounding woods, leaving brushstrokes of quicksilver on every leaf and bush. Deena missed the peonies in their organza ball gowns, now just a memory, but standing proudly at the ready were French hydrangeas coming into their own. "Don't

17

worry," they seemed to say. "We'll take it from here." Too bad the pretty little impatiens and petunias hadn't been planted. The annuals were usually in by now. If she wanted to enjoy them again she'd better get busy.

Her parents would have loved it here. Deena liked to imagine them meeting Simon, coming to their wedding, driving up for visits. If they'd been around, her time with Agatha wouldn't have devolved into a one-sided boxing match. The truth was, Simon had a point. She had spent years providing concierge service to an ungrateful, bitter woman. Every once in a while he'd ask why she hung in. His question would prompt Deena to insist that she loved her aunt . . . which hadn't been the case for years. It wasn't even an inherited Middle Eastern morality that kept her going back for more.

It was regret—the companion of choice on any guilt trip. Deena had spent the last thirty years making up for the actions of her twenty-five-year-old self. She couldn't rewrite history. Her parents were dead. The best she could hope for now was to make sure she didn't repeat the same mistakes.

And there was something more—something Simon couldn't appreciate because he'd never seen it. Her aunt had taken an insecure, awkward fifteen-year-old and, over the course of countless weekend visits, exposed her to everything New York had to offer—theaters, restaurants, museums, nightlife. If not for Agatha, Deena would have ended up in a nothing job, away from the stage, in the bowels of blue-collar Philadelphia.

No matter how ungrateful and, yes, abusive her aunt had become, she wouldn't abandon her now.

4

1969

"Deena, for God's sake, don't you see where you are?"

Agatha and Deena were sitting in Maxwell's Plum, the latest Manhattan hotspot. The newly reopened Maxwell's was extravagant. Stained-glass windows on the walls and ceiling, large dining room, Tiffany lamps. Art Nouveau on steroids. "Marrakesh Express" was playing on the sound system, mingled with the chatter of the crowd's exhilaration at being in the right place at the right time.

"Sure I do, Aunt Agatha," stammered a fifteen-year-old Deena.

Agatha sat at the table with a cigarette in her hand, scotch at the ready.

Deena loved the way her aunt knew the best places to go and the perfect clothes to wear. She wasn't exactly beautiful, but that didn't seem to bother her. Anybody could see that she loved who she was.

"Jesus," said Agatha, "we're sitting in *the* restaurant in New York and you're afraid to look left or right. Have you noticed who's sitting two tables over? Warren Beatty. You *did* see *Bonnie and Clyde*, didn't you?"

Deena tried to look to her right without moving her head, but her bird's nest of black hair, frizzy and unkempt, made it nearly impossible. Her mother was always telling her to brush her hair away from her face so that people could see her dark eyes, but Deena thought her forehead was way too high and her nose way too big. She watched the rail-thin miniskirted women and long-haired men in flowered shirts standing three deep at the bar exchanging all manner of pills and potions while she sat there like a lump wearing a shapeless brown dress, feeling like the ugliest girl in the world. She wanted to die.

She'd arrived from Philadelphia the day before. It was her first trip to the big city, and she was excited to be staying with her aunt. She loved her parents, sure, but there was nobody as worldly as Aunt Agatha. What she admired most was that her aunt had escaped Philadelphia just four years before and was already living a dream life. Deena wished she had half of Aunt Agatha's courage, but how was that going to happen when she was teased at school every day? Deena-da-dog. That's what they called her.

Maybe someday she'd move to New York. She'd have weekends just like this whenever she wanted, enjoying dinners in fancy restaurants and going to Broadway shows. Last night they went to *Hair* and at the end of Act I there were naked people actually onstage! She could never tell her father.

Agatha lit another cigarette with an elegant flourish. Deena loved watching her expressive hands—Agatha's one beautiful feature. Deena used to play with those long, tapered fingers when she was younger, touching her aunt's nails, tapping them as if they were keys on a piano. Agatha kept them forever posed, always graceful, the fingers never bent too much, the lines of her hands in an elegant curve. They performed their own pas de deux during a conversation, lighting a cigarette, hailing a cab.

"So what would you like for dinner?" asked Agatha, taking another sip from her scotch.

Deena surveyed the huge menu. Making a choice was fraught with danger. Some things she recognized, others not at all. She was surprised to see hamburgers on the list, but she could never order that. What would Aunt Agatha say? But sweetbreads and quenelles and tarte Tatin were complete mysteries.

The waiter was coming and she felt panic grab at her stomach. She had to make a decision.

"May I take your order?" asked the waiter, with a friendly smile.

This was it. Deena avoided Agatha's eyes, took a breath, and said, "I'll have . . . the frog legs."

5

After breakfast, Deena gave Kayla Madden a call. When the teenager answered, Deena did her best to stifle a sigh. She really liked Kayla—could even identify with the girl's painful shyness—but, my goodness, her timid *hello* was barely audible. Deena had to remind herself that, once upon a time, she'd suffered from the same insecurities—until, that is, she'd mastered the conjuring act of a new personality with the wave of an actor's hand. She suspected that Kayla would learn to do the same.

They exchanged a few pleasantries, after which Deena offered Kayla her working copies of *Hamlet* and *Othello*. Shakespeare was a requirement for college theater programs. They were just arranging where to meet when Deena heard the cigarette rasp of a voice yelling in the background.

"For fuck's sake, put that phone away."

It was Kayla's mother. Jesus. No wonder the kid was quiet.

"Umm," said a flustered Kayla, "I, umm, better go."

"Let's meet at the theater," said Deena. "Say, eleven-thirty? I'll have those plays for you and we can settle on a schedule."

Deena could hear another missile launch in the background. "I said, get off your goddam phone!"

Kayla mumbled "I'll see you there" and quickly ended the call.

Damn. It was hard enough being a teenager without a screaming parent monkeying up the works. This small slice of Kayla's home life made Deena doubly impressed with the job she'd done in *Junior Miss* at the Brixton Playhouse last year. The role of Judy Graves was the center of the show. Deena had needed to cast someone with a natural sense of humor, half-kid, half-adult, and against all logic, Kayla had nailed it.

Deena kept her complete set of Shakespeare on a bookshelf in the living room, but her working copy of *Hamlet* was at the theater, and her *Othello* was packed away in the attic. She piled her breakfast dishes in the sink and went up to the second floor.

When she pulled down the attic staircase and started her climb, she was met with a thick wall of heat. And with each step, Deena crossed into another time zone.

It's easy to forget an attic. It sits quietly on top of the house like a net, catching whatever memories threaten to float away. When a renegade story from the past wanders into a person's field of vision, it's the attic that provides a place to go and visit and remember.

Deena pulled the chain hanging from the single bare lightbulb, bringing the palette of blacks and grays into focus. But when she stepped into the room, she felt suddenly lightheaded—as if the attic was holding its breath. She steadied herself with a quick grab of the rafter as she tossed off her imagination, chalking her dizziness up to the heat.

Stacks of boxes, furniture, and moldering trunks were tucked into every corner. Deena walked in and around them as her hand brushed through the drapery of cobwebs covering an abandoned cityscape of back-in-the-day, its phantoms hiding in shadows waiting to be remembered, hoping to be found.

As she pulled her hair into a ponytail, her eyes moved to a plastic storage container filled with her parents' belongings. Deena couldn't resist taking a look. She lifted the lid to find a pretty little box from her mother's bureau sitting on top of a pile of books. She had no idea what was in it. Thirty years ago she'd barely finished packing up her parents' house before the movers were there, knocking at the door. The idea of checking inside boxes and bags hadn't even been on the menu.

She reached for the five-by-six-inch box, excited to see what was inside. But as her fingers touched the lid an encore from the rehab center blew into the room. A woman's whisper. And it was saying, *Ahhh.*

Deena jerked her hand away. The air pushed against her chest as she did a quick scan of the room.

Get a grip, she thought. It was the attic's gloom playing tricks on her, or maybe a breeze blowing against the gable's round window.

Deena gave her head a shake, picked up the box, and tried to lift the lid, but found it locked. She put it by the attic hatch with a plan to work on it later.

She eventually came to her theater boxes, their tops dressed in a thick layer of dust and their labels rippled with damp. Deena couldn't help but backburner her search for the *Othello* as she sat on one of the crates and reached for the file box labeled REVIEWS.

Her first glimpse inside brought her back to the rainy November afternoon in 2001 when she and Simon were packing their apartment into ever-multiplying boxes. They hadn't wanted to leave Manhattan, but Tribeca was too close to the 9/11 attack for comfort. It was supposed to be a temporary move, and yet, here they were, years later, with no plans to move back.

She pulled out the first folder, releasing spores of mold that had been trapped within the papers' fibers. They rose up like a cloud, coating her throat with the cloying taste of musty earth. Deena brushed the dirt from her hands and wiped the sweat from her upper lip before removing a fistful of clippings from the *Times,* the *New*

Yorker, the *Post.* Yellow-highlighted phrases were scattered here and there like trinkets, gifts, little baubles to gather up and hug tightly to her breast . . . *fresh young talent* . . . *GRIPPING* . . . *excels as Minnie.*

Now she was in it. Next came her box of headshots and costume photos. There she was as Sofya in *Uncle Vanya,* Jenny in *Nelly's Hell,* Emily in *Our Town.* Deena had never been a classic beauty, but there had always been something in her eyes that came through in a photo. Something that said, "You'll be happy to know me."

She looked wistfully at the collection, struck by how young she was. *To have one more run,* she thought. *One last ride on the merry-go-round.*

When Deena looked up, she caught her reflection in a mirror propped up against an old dresser. The unforgiving shadows cast by the attic's bare lightbulb brought her under-eye circles and careworn face to the fore. She couldn't resist placing her fingertips on either side of her jaw and gently pushing her jowls back, transforming her reflection into an approximation of the girl she once was. With a sigh she looked back at her headshots. *Where did it all go?*

Deena set aside her self-indulgence as she put the costume shots back in their folder and then reached for the file box. But before she could pull the box closer she heard something inside, trying to get out. This wasn't some imagined voice. One of the file folders had moved.

She jumped to her feet and inched away, keeping her eyes on the folders. Then, in her peripheral vision, she caught a sudden movement, something darting across the floor. Deena took in a startled breath as a mouse skittered from the box's chewed-out corner and ran across her foot.

Jesus! That's it. I'm outta here.

She jammed the photos back into the file box and quickly found her plays. Then she tucked *Othello* under her arm, grabbed the little locked box, and left the attic with its unsettling sounds and surprises behind her.

It was just past eleven when Deena got to the theater, a large converted barn with a gambrel roof. There was a banner above the sliding front doors with *Brixton Playhouse* laid out in bright red letters and WAY OFF BROADWAY printed below. A community theater like this was rare, with permanent seating for the audience and a proper backstage equipped with all the fixin's. Brixton was one of the reasons she and Simon had chosen Stanhope.

Deena went around to the stage door, let herself in, and turned on the lights. She then walked out onto the stage—her way of saying "Back again" to the ghosts of productions past. It felt good to be home. Whenever she walked on those boards her lungs expanded and her head lifted up off her shoulders. There was nothing better than an empty theater. If you stood center stage and looked out over the house, you could just about see the shadows of past performances dipping and swirling above the empty seats. Deena never lost sight of how lucky she was to be there. After years of debilitating panic attacks, Brixton had given her back the life she'd lost. Thank God those years had passed.

With her obligatory visit to the stage done, she headed to the green room. The hallway was even more stifling than the attic. Again she sensed a holding of breath—this time within the confines of the darkened corridor. Deena gathered her hair into a bun and fanned her neck, but it didn't do much good.

When she reached the green room she turned on the light and headed to the corner bookshelf, bursting with scripts. Her copy of *Hamlet* was jammed between *The Play That Goes Wrong* and *Fat Pig*—not the most dignified place for the Prince of Denmark. With play in hand she plopped down on the beat-up couch with its nonexistent springs and thumbed through the dog-eared pages. It was fun to read the barely legible notes she'd scrawled along the margins. Deena had never played Ophelia professionally, but she'd—

What was that tapping?

She put down the *Othello* and went to the open door. "Kayla? Is that you?"

Her voice echoed back to her as the lights gave a quick flicker. Deena peered down the hall trying to figure out where the tapping was coming from, but it soon stopped. With a shrug she turned back into the room. As she stepped away from the door, a hum, low and drone-like, emerged from within the darkened corridor. Or was it a voice?

It was both—as if the voice and the hum were skipping down the hall, arm in arm, dancing toward the green room. And just like in the attic, it was saying *Ahhhhh*.

No, wait. It was, *I-I-I-I-I've . . .*

"Hello?" Her stomach tightened into a fist as she looked back at the open door. "Is that you, Kayla?"

Deena wiped away a trickle of sweat traveling down her forehead as she took a step backwards into the room. The voice quietly laughed as it got closer.

"I-I-I-I-I've got you . . ."

What? thought Deena. *What did it say?*

A stack of books sitting on a side table suddenly fell to the floor with a loud *whap*. Deena spun toward the sound, nervously scanning the shadows for an intruder, but there was none. Her right hand started shaking.

With a subtle lowering of temperature the laughter from the hall entered the room, billowing past her, catching her hair in its draft. Deena's hand was now shaking in earnest. She grabbed it with her left, trying to get it under control.

"I-I-I-I-I've got you now."

"Who are you?" yelled Deena, squaring her shoulders as she marshaled what little courage she could. "What do you want?"

The laughter bounced around the room like a taunting child, teasing, needling, until it settled behind her, blocking Deena's escape. The hum rose higher in pitch, piercing the stale, hot air. Deena threw her hands over her ears hoping to block it out—which was when she discovered it wasn't coming from the room. It was coming from inside her head, growing louder and higher, throbbing against her temples, pressing against her eyes until it felt as if they would burst from their sockets. Her teeth joined in the assault, doubling her pain. A drop of blood hit her shirt. Jesus. Her nose was bleeding.

Make it stop, she thought desperately, as if there was a guard or hall monitor ready to step in and save the day.

She heard footsteps coming from the corridor.

Coming closer.

Deena was trapped in the green room with no way out. She tightened the grip over her ears, but it did no good. Then ... a hand?—my God, a *hand* touched her shoulder.

"No!" she cried. Her shoulders flew up. "Don't—"

"Mrs. Bartlett?"

Deena's eyes shot open. *Kayla*. Deena struggled to come back to herself as she lowered her arms and turned around.

"Gee, Mrs. Bartlett. I didn't mean to scare you."

6

Deena's meeting with Kayla was like a poorly synchronized film, the subtitles saying one thing, the actor's lips another. Between her internal replay of what had just happened in the green room, coupled with Kayla's not-so-subtle looks of concern, it was surprising they managed to nail down a summer coaching schedule at all.

The *I've got you now* voice had to be imagined, right? If it had been real, Kayla would have heard it as well. Buildings were living, breathing beasts waiting for a susceptible person to assign motives to random snaps, crackles, and pops. Tapping pipes. Drafty hallways. Creaking, clanking, knocking, squeaking. Fodder for an overactive imagination. Added to that was Simon's constant warning weighing on her mind, putting that imagination into overdrive.

But what about the blood?

Deena checked the front of her shirt where she remembered a tiny rosebud of blood forming during the worst of the assault. It was clean. For a quick second she wondered if Simon was right. Maybe she was headed into trouble. Maybe . . .

No. She was fine. Just fine.

They decided on Thursday afternoons for their sessions. Deena may have understood Kayla's shyness, but the teenager's inability to look her in the eye was beginning to wear thin. There was just so much Deena was willing to abide if it dredged up too many memories of her own awkward years.

Once their schedule was set, it was time to head to Wilshire. Maybe when she got there the cramped feeling in her stomach would unwind.

———

A half-hour later she was walking down Wilshire's second-floor corridor, happy to put disembodied voices in empty theaters behind her. But the day hadn't finished with her. Deena spied the old cleaning lady from yesterday twenty feet down the hall, rolling her cart in Deena's direction.

Jesus. I don't need this right now.

The woman had the side-to-side gait of a person with arthritic hips, although it didn't seem to bother her. It was as if she had harnessed the air under her feet to gently push each step forward. Their eyes met and the woman smiled. Deena braced for another premonition, but the woman kept walking, mumbling something as she passed.

When Deena reached the nurses' station, she motioned for one of them to come over.

"Yes, Mrs. Bartlett, what can I do for you?"

"I was curious. See that old cleaning lady over there?"

"You mean Jadwiga? Sure."

"She said the strangest thing to me yesterday. I was wondering about her."

"I wouldn't pay her any mind. Jadwiga may be an odd duck, but she's harmless. Been working at the Center since the eighties. Every once in a while she takes a shine to one of the patients, but she never oversteps. Poor thing lost most of her family twenty-five years ago to, of all things, the flu. At least that's the current story. Jadwiga-lore changes regularly. What did she say to you?"

"Oh, nothing," said Deena, fiddling with the strap of her handbag. "Thanks for the info." She gave the nurse a parting smile and turned toward Agatha's room.

As the heels of her sandals quietly clicked along the corridor, Deena was struck by the bleakness of it all. It was as if an arcane, poorly reasoned law had banned the use of hardwood floors and mandated that the hallway be papered in a sickening shade of green. She counted off the rooms as she went, each doorway an entrance into another person's life with its own brand of hopelessness draped on the walls surrounding their bed.

Deena neared her aunt's room and straightened up, bracing for another day of waiting, another day of watching. But when she walked in, she was surprised by a visitor.

"Lucine," said Deena. "You came."

Agatha's friend Lucine Saud stood up from her chair and rushed over.

"Of course I did," she said, stepping in for a hug, bringing with her the shared experience of their Syrian background with its rules, expectations, and, yes, joy. Here was someone who understood where Deena came from because she came from the same place.

Deena leaned into Lucine's body, breathing in the floral-scented powder so prevalent among women of a certain age.

"How could I not come?" said Lucine. "Agatha and I have known each other for fifty years." And then she cried.

Deena pulled up a chair and they sat together holding hands while Agatha lay in bed, sleeping. After a minute or two Lucine blew her nose and turned toward Deena.

"Look at you. How long has it been—ten years?"

"Nearly twelve."

"I'm so sorry I haven't been here to help. I expect you've had your hands full."

Deena understood better than anyone why Lucine hadn't come. Alienating friends was Agatha's stock-in-trade. She gave Lucine a reassuring smile and said, "It's okay. I get it. But I won't lie, it's been tough. You know how difficult Aunt Agatha can be."

Lucine gave a small laugh and nodded. "I *was* surprised she ended up at that assisted living facility after her apartment fire. I have several friends living there, and from what I've seen, it's not exactly Agatha's style."

"It was her own fault. I'd lined up a much nicer place . . . until Aunt Agatha blew it up."

"Blew it up? How?"

"She didn't pass the interview. A rep from The Valley asked her what had set off the apartment fire and Aunt Agatha, the most honest person in the world, told her it started with the cigarette she'd been smoking in bed."

"That must have raised an eyebrow."

"It gets better. The interviewer made some crack about creative ways a person stops smoking, to which Aunt Agatha said, 'Who says I'm stopping?'"

"Oh, no."

"Oh, yes. So, I quickly pointed out that she wouldn't be allowed to smoke. She whipped her head in my direction and said, 'Cut the bullshit. On what planet would a woman my age stop smoking?'"

"Oh, God. I know where this is going."

Deena nodded. "The next day I got a call from The Valley rescinding their offer. Aunt Agatha was 'a danger to herself and others.'"

"That's horrible. What did Agatha say when you told her?"

Deena grimaced. "I didn't just tell her. I called her at the hospital and screamed it to her. It had taken weeks of research and interviews and visits to find The Valley, and she flushed it down the toilet. Honestly, Lucine, I just lost control."

"And Agatha?"

"Didn't say a word. When I was finished she simply hung up. Next time we spoke, it was as if nothing had happened."

"That's Aggie. Unmoving. Never changing."

Deena gave a short laugh. "You said it."

The memory of that day still rattled its chains. It hadn't been easy finding an assisted living place with the kind of amenities her aunt demanded. In addition to The Valley's generously sized rooms and hotel-like lobby, it had three restaurants and a little movie theater. It would have been perfect.

Deena felt the room closing in. She had to get away from the sight of her aunt.

"How about a cup of coffee?" she said to Lucine.

"Sure."

They went to the lounge, grabbed their coffees, and settled into a pair of mismatched armchairs by a large picture window. The lounge had the feel of a college meeting room with its linoleum floor and used furniture—a final stage set for the bookending of an adult life, starting and finishing with other people's castaways.

"You know, Agatha never used to be difficult." Lucine stared down at her cup. "Zahra and Agatha Haddad," she remembered. "They were the center of everything. Your mother was the pretty one. Beautiful eyes, thick wavy hair. Personality to match—lovely inside and out. Agatha was the feisty one. Full of fun. Ready for anything. Fiercely loyal. They were devoted to each other. Then sometime in the fifties, there was a rift. Aggie was never the same."

"Nobody ever told me this. What happened?"

"I don't know. This was before your aunt and I became friends. Years later, when I asked her about it, she refused to talk, which always struck me as sad. Their falling out was clearly painful for both of them, but Agatha had turned that pain into anger. It eventually drove most of her friends away."

"Except you," said Deena.

"I hung in as long as I could. Our relationship was cemented when we found ourselves in New York together. I'd moved—let me see—in '63. Agatha followed a couple years later. We were close."

"Until Aunt Agatha boarded her bus to Ugly Town."

Lucine laughed. "That's one way of putting it." She reached for Deena's hand. "What always surprised me was not only Agatha's relationship with you, but Zahra's willingness to allow it. Maybe it was their way of forging a path back. If your mother hadn't died, they may have succeeded."

Why didn't Deena know this story? It opened up so many questions. She would give anything to ask her mother, or even Agatha, what had happened.

But her mother was dead.

And Agatha was Agatha.

Deena and Lucine went back to her aunt's room, where they reminisced about happy times, shared histories, golden memories of people long gone. Lucine cried. Deena cried. Agatha slept.

After another half-hour there was movement from the bed. As Agatha's eyes slowly opened, Lucine pulled her chair close, leaned in, and said, "Hello, Aggie. It's me." She gave Agatha a smile and took her hand. "How are you doing, my old friend?"

Agatha stared at Lucine for a few seconds until, with a croak, she said, "What the hell are you doing here?"

Lucine blanched at the refrain of Agatha's favorite tune. She took an involuntary breath and inched away as Agatha went back to sleep.

Poor Lucine, thought Deena. *She doesn't deserve this*. Deena placed a reassuring hand on her shoulder and they sat in silence for a few more minutes.

When it was time for Lucine to go, she gave Deena a hug. "You've had a tough time," she said. "If your mother was alive, things might've been easier. Just remember who you are. Beautiful. Talented. Devoted. If you ever need anything, call."

After she left, Deena lowered herself into a chair with her eyes tightly closed. Lucine's visit had ushered in the past, bringing with it the specter of her mother's emaciated body, laid out before her like an indictment. The phone calls Deena had left unreturned, the bad excuses for not going home, and then, a week before her mother died, finally showing up at her bedside. Deena had told herself she'd been absent because she couldn't face her mother's cancer, but that was a lie.

Philadelphia was where her insecurity lived. Deena was ashamed of who she used to be—teased and lonely and fearful. She had turned her back on all of it when she'd moved to Manhattan two years earlier. She was an actor now, a New Yorker. A completely different person. Not only had her Philadelphia visits grown further apart, but she'd hardly ever called home. When her mother got sick Deena figured she was only fifty. She'd get better. And then, one Sunday afternoon, her father called to say that time was short.

Her mother had looked impossibly small lying there with her sunken cheeks, her beautiful hair nearly gone, and her eyes, once so gentle, so expressive, staring at death. All she'd wanted was to spend the last months of her life with Deena by her side. But by the time Deena arrived, her mother had barely recognized her, could hardly speak. She had denied her mother the one gift that was within her power to give: the solace of her company.

But the object lesson was wasted. A week after the funeral she boarded a train back to New York, leaving her father alone in that empty house. He hadn't asked her to stay longer, but the surprise on his face when she announced her plans had said it all. And still Deena left, thinking only about returning to her New York life.

Three weeks later he was dead. If she had been there, she could have performed CPR until the EMTs arrived. She might have even gotten him to the hospital herself. If all that had failed, at least she would have been by her father's side as he slipped away. He wouldn't have died alone.

Well done, Deena.

7

Deena coasted into her driveway and sat in the front seat, watching Simon as he added mulch to the flowerbeds. She hated to leave the car's safe harbor after the day she'd had. Lucine's visit had roused a collection of memories that was still circling overhead. And then, of course, there was the theater and that imagined voice. Years of instability made it easy to believe there was a monster under the bed. Even a healthy dose of therapy couldn't stop old juggernauts from starting their engines.

She almost wished the voice had been real. If paranoia became her new hobby, those old panic attacks would seem like inconsequential wrinkles in her timeline.

Simon spotted her in the driveway and walked up to the car with a wide grin.

"How about a kiss?" he said, as Deena rolled down the window.

"Sure. I love me a sweaty man."

He came in for a kiss, bringing the smell of the garden with him. Then he straightened up and with hands on hips, said, "I think that warrants a decent dinner."

"Maybe yes, maybe no. It all depends on how you leave my petunia beds."

"Okay, fine. But after that much work, I should get dinner *and* a raise."

"I'll be the judge of that."

Simon pulled a plucked dandelion from his pocket and wedged it behind her ear, and with a wink, got back to work.

Deena grabbed the grocery bags from the trunk and went into the house.

The kitchen was stifling. She left her bags on the farmhouse table, turned on the AC, and looked to Spotify for a bit of music. *Tom Waits seems about right*, she thought, perusing her playlist.

As "Table Top Joe" started up, Deena focused on dinner. She'd just dumped the vegetables out onto the butcher-block island when her eyes fell on the little box she'd rescued from the attic. The carved wood and leather inlay looked so pretty sitting there on the kitchen counter. She could remember Saturday afternoons with her mother, going through the treasures in her bureau drawer, jewelry mostly. But for some reason this box was off limits.

Not anymore.

She shoved the vegetables aside, took the box off the counter, and placed it on the island next to a pile of red peppers. Then, grabbing a butter knife, Deena squared off for her best impression of a thief jimmying a lock. But before the knife even touched the box, the lid sprang open.

What the hell? It was locked. I know it was.

She stared at the open box for a second or two as she pulled one of the stools over to the island and sat down. It was foolish to be startled by such a little thing. She changed her focus onto what was inside.

A pile of black-and-white photos lay on top of several unopened letters. The photos had the scalloped edge that photographers used once upon a time—and the top photo was an eye-popper. A teenage version of her mother was laughing as she tried to protect her head from a garden hose spewing a fountain of water. The hose was wielded by her younger sister, Agatha, while Deena's grandfather stood with a wide grin, his pants hiked up over his big belly and a pipe clenched in his teeth. Agatha looked to be nine years old. That would have made her mother fourteen.

God, they were young. And Agatha was actually laughing.

There were several more photos, each capturing a slice of a happy family's life. Blowing out candles at a birthday party. Doing the *Dabke*, a Syrian circle dance, at their cousin's wedding. Sitting with Teta around the kitchen table, making stuffed grape leaves. Each photo more joyful than the last.

But when Deena reached the letters a very different picture came into focus. All but one was from her mother, unopened and marked *Return to Sender*.

Deena grabbed the first letter and opened it.

September 3, 1965

Aggie:
> *You can't keep hanging up when I call. Please.*
> *Let's talk. We're sisters. And I love you.*

Love,
Zahra
xoxo

And the next:

January 15, 1966

Aggie:
> *What can I do, my darling, to make things*
> *right? A one-day visit on Christmas isn't the*

way to spend a holiday. Even Momma noticed
you weren't talking to me. Call me. Please.

Love,
Zahra
xoxo

P.S. I'm enclosing a picture of Deena. I hope
you like it. She asks about you all the time.

There were three more, all begging Agatha to call, but the one that really caught Deena's attention was an already-open envelope with a one-page letter Agatha had written back to her mother. Actually, it wasn't a letter; it was four simple words:

STOP CALLING. STOP WRITING.

The four-word missive was classic Agatha. Implacable. Stubborn. Abrupt. To see the unopened letters next to the old photos reinforced the question Deena couldn't help but ask. What in the world could have happened to have turned fun-loving Agatha into the woman Deena had come to know?

Her unanswered question was interrupted by the sweet smell of perfume . . . gardenias and lilacs and jasmine. The perfume's fragrance brought with it a collection of memories tied up with a ribbon and offered as a gift. White Shoulders—her mother's favorite. Deena remembered crawling onto her mother's lap where the scent of White Shoulders was waiting to wrap her in a quilt of flowers.

She reflexively turned her head, half expecting to see her mother standing behind her, ready to kiss her cheek and smooth her hair. Of course there was no one there. She checked to see if the smell had come from the wooden box, but no.

Damn it. Maybe the self-opening box had fired Deena's imagination. That had to be it.

She folded the letters, slipped them into their envelopes, and put everything back in the box. With her trove of letters and pictures set aside, she finally got busy with dinner. It was a relief to do something normal.

Before long, two arms grabbed her from behind.

"Gotcha," said Simon.

"The happy gardener returns."

He nuzzled his unshaven face in the crook of her neck. "I'm a hungry workin' man. When will dinner be ready?"

"Fifteen minutes," she said, reaching behind to give Simon a playful pinch at the waist.

He jumped back. "Hey. Watch it."

Deena turned to face him. He was wearing an old pair of shorts, wellies, and that tattered T-shirt of his with Che Guevara printed on the front. She took hold of his cheeks with both hands and gave him a big smack on the lips. "Now, if you could see your way to washing off half the dirt in Stanhope, I could use a gin and tonic."

"You got it, darlin'."

When he came back, he was met with a collection of bowls and pans lying in a battlefield of vegetable peelings scattered around the counter and dropping on the floor.

"God," he said. "You're a gorilla in the kitchen."

She laughed. "It's my process. Embrace it."

After making her a drink, Simon set the table and pulled out a bottle of wine. Deena sensed him watching—a leftover from their talk this morning—but she chose to ignore it. She finished her pre-dinner gin and tonic with a final gulp, raised the glass above her head, and jiggled the ice—the universal signal for a refill. Simon obliged.

When dinner was finally ready, they sat down and dug in to their pasta primavera.

If mealtime didn't exist, someone would have to invent another way for people to kibitz about their day. There's nothing better than adding a thought or story to a dinner table's bounty.

Deena showed Simon her mother's box of treasures and, of course, he wasn't surprised that there'd been a falling-out. Then, after sharing his day, he grabbed a second helping of pasta and said, "What about Kayla? Have you reached out?"

A veil came down on Deena's good mood as she remembered the *I've got you now* voice in the theater. She'd been wrestling all day over whether to tell Simon about it, but the *should-I, shouldn't-I* game was leaning toward no. The fact remained that her darling husband was a bloodhound looking for any reason to see her back in therapy.

Deena decided to keep her mouth shut. It didn't make sense to get Simon worked up over an isolated figment of her imagination. So . . . one point scored for the *shouldn't-I* team.

She took a sip of her wine. "You'll be happy to know that not only did I speak with Kayla, but we met at the theater and arranged a coaching schedule."

"That's great news! This calls for a celebration. Bundle yourself in the living room and wait for me while I clean up this unholy mess you've made. I have a surprise for you."

"Hmm . . . and what might that be?"

"Oh, ye with little patience. You'll have to wait. Now, off with you."

Deena headed to the living room with its floor-to-ceiling bookcases, wide-board floors, and welcoming fireplace. It was their favorite spot in the house. In the winter they'd light a fire and wrap themselves in the cozy merino blanket that was kept draped over the back of the couch. Deena would have enjoyed the comfort of it if the summer night wasn't so warm.

There was an eclectic collection of artwork on the walls that had no rhyme or reason. A Led Zeppelin poster next to a Chagall litho next to a framed prayer rug. Simon would have preferred something more organized, but Deena would regularly sabotage his efforts with some crazy something she dragged home like a stray puppy. Their collection was a perfect example of who they were—an incongruous couple that somehow worked.

She curled up on the couch waiting for Simon to finish. This was exactly what Deena needed. A relaxing night away from Agatha worries. She was just nodding off when she felt Simon beside her, giving one of his famous foot rubs.

"Wakey, wakey," he said.

Deena stretched and with a laugh, said, "It's about time." Then she thrust out her hand and added, "Gimme."

"Not so fast. Close your eyes."

She crossed her legs under her and did a quick bounce before closing her eyes. Simon milked the moment for all it was worth, pretending to put something in her hand, tickling her foot, grabbing her nose. In retaliation Deena threatened to bite his ear, which earned her two small pieces of paper placed in her open palms.

"Okay," said Simon. "Open."

Her lips circled into an O as she looked down to find two tickets for *War Horse* at the Vivian Beaumont. She'd been dying to go, but with all that had been happening with Agatha, they hadn't managed it. Now that *War Horse* had won a Tony last year, seats were impossible to come by.

"How did you get them? And when are we going—Tuesday night? Oh, Simon!"

"We're gonna have a ball, and Lord knows we need it. Morrie and Jill had two extra tickets, so we'll meet them for an early dinner and then, because nothing is too good for my sweetheart, we'll stay at the Mandarin Oriental after the show."

"Oh, I love you! I can't wait!"

Deena hadn't felt excited about a night out in ages. She grabbed Simon by the collar and pulled him close.

"Now, if I were you," she whispered, with her lips close to his ear, "I'd take advantage of the situation, 'cause the only thing better than make up sex is gratitude sex. And sweetheart . . ." She lightly bit his earlobe. "I'm grateful."

They didn't bother going upstairs. They threw the back cushions off the couch and tussled and wrestled till they couldn't. Happy and sated, they quickly fell asleep.

———

At two a.m., Deena bolted upright, woken out of a dead sleep by a sound. The whispered voice from the theater?

Oh, Jesus. Please no.

A beam of light from the full moon shone through the windows, wedging dark shadows into every corner. They dug themselves in and then jutted toward the couch where she lay. She scanned the room, listening, but it was quiet.

Deena glanced at Simon, still asleep against the back of the couch, thank God. He'd been harping about her exhaustion for weeks, and the last thing she needed was another third degree.

As if the thought of that conversation was enough to summon exhaustion from the ether, Deena suddenly felt a deep weariness come over her—the kind that stripped away the muscles in her arms and legs, turning them into useless sacks of flesh. She'd never felt this kind of fatigue. It was so intense that, if she surrendered, her body would disintegrate into the cushions, seep down through the couch, and fall out of sight. Deena did her best to ignore it, refocusing her attention on the room for one last check. She held her breath and listened.

Nothing.

She must have dreamt it. That had to be it.

Deena shouldn't have been surprised that she was imagining things. The past year had taken its toll. Just as she'd dipped her toe back into acting, Agatha had bitten it off. All of her plans had to be put on hold so she could focus on an apartment fire that kicked off a bumper-car ride of switchbacks and dead-ends. A visit to rehab for smoke inhalation. A hard-fought search for an assisted living facility, blown up. A panicked scramble for a replacement. Then, just when it looked as if Agatha was settled, an emergency trip to the hospital for her heart, with sepsis fueling her last stop—Wilshire.

Everyone faces age with the hope that there will be someone by their side, easing the journey. She and Agatha may have had a rocky start, but after years of regular visits they had finally become close—so close, in fact, that moving to New York had been Agatha's idea.

Deena had loved her aunt once upon a time, and she knew her aunt had loved her in return, which made where they now stood that much more a mystery. There was even a night long ago when, in Agatha's darkest hour, Deena had offered comfort. And while Agatha hadn't told Deena the full story behind her distress, she did something far more courageous: She let Deena see her pain. It was the closest they had ever been.

After all the cruel words she'd suffered, Deena wished she could go back to the days when spending an evening with Agatha wasn't a chore or a burden—when it was like being with a good friend.

8

1977

Deena stood at her aunt's door, her finger poised over the doorbell, and a monster duffel bag by her side. After all the planning, all the dreaming, she was finally moving to Manhattan. Gone was the naive fifteen-year-old who'd made her first visit to New York eight years before. In her place was a twenty-three-year-old actor with an open face and a determined walk.

Agatha greeted her with a cigarette in her perfectly manicured hand. She gave Deena a hug, holding her a little longer than expected. If Deena hadn't known her aunt better, she might have thought Agatha was softening up. Even though they'd become close over the past few years, her aunt rarely showed affection.

"Come in," she said. "You're early."

"I hope that's okay," said Deena.

"Of course it is. I was just about to take a nap. Make yourself at home."

Agatha disappeared into the bedroom while Deena went to the kitchen, poured herself an iced tea, and hunkered down with the *Times*. Her aunt had promised to get Deena a few auditions for some downtown showcases—she knew a lot of people in the business—but that wasn't going to get Deena a place to live. There just had to be a job and apartment waiting for her in the neatly columned ads of the *Times* classifieds.

Her aunt stayed in the bedroom for hours. At 8:30 p.m. she reappeared wearing a robe and slippers with an ever-present cigarette in her hand. Not wanting to brave the summer heat, they ordered up from Wang Fu's.

They were just finishing when the lights in the apartment went out.

"Christ," said Agatha, exasperated. "We must have blown a fuse." She flicked on her lighter and lit two candles. Without air-conditioning the room was already feeling warm. Deena happened to glance out the window and did a double take.

"Aunt Agatha, look. It's completely dark outside."

Sure enough, every building, every streetlight—the entire city was black except for a string of cars and buses shining their headlights along Fifth Avenue, looking for all the world like Chinese New Year dragons dancing in the dark.

There was a knock at the door. "Miss Haddad. It's Victor."

Agatha opened the door for the building super standing there with a lit flashlight in his hand. "What's going on, Victor?"

"It's a citywide blackout. We may be in the dark for a while."

"Jesus."

"If you need anything, use your phone to call the front desk. The intercom isn't working."

"Will do. Thanks for coming up."

Agatha slammed the door. "God damn this city." She strode into the living room and sat on the couch opposite Deena. "We're drowning in garbage, stores are going out of business, and now *this*."

47

There was a catch in her aunt's voice.

"Are you okay?" asked Deena.

Agatha stared at the space in front of her as she fidgeted with her cigarette lighter. "That, my dear, is a question best saved for another day. But I will say this: The cesspool that New York has turned into matches my disaster of a life."

Something caught Deena's eye in the dim light. *Are those tears on Aunt Agatha's face?*

Couldn't be. They were beads of sweat from the rising temperature in the apartment.

Hold on.

Yes.

They were tears.

Deena was struck dumb. This wasn't her aunt. Not by a long shot.

Agatha quickly brushed them away and took a long drag from the last of her cigarette.

Deena felt embarrassed by her aunt's momentary lapse of control. Rather than look at her, she chose to watch the cigarette smoke coiling like a gossamer scarf toward the candle's flame. When she finally hazarded a look back, their eyes met—and what she saw shocked her. Agatha's slightly pulled back lower lip and softened eyes showed an uncharacteristic vulnerability, the antithesis of everything Deena had come to know about her aunt.

"It's Michael," said Agatha, quickly looking away.

Michael had been her aunt's boyfriend for nine years, an unlikely lady's man, paunchy with thinning hair, large nose, and thick glasses. The one thing he had going for him was his love of women, and because of that, women couldn't help but love him in return.

Oh, and he was married.

"What happened?" said Deena.

Agatha looked back at Deena, clearly struggling with whether to tell her. Maybe she was wondering if Deena could be trusted. They'd been close, but it was always Deena looking to Agatha for advice, not the other way around.

Agatha sat up a little straighter and said, "Let's just say that Michael and I have reached a parting of the ways."

"Oh my God, Aunt Agatha. I'm so sorry."

It was that simple show of sympathy that broke her. This time the tears flowed freely as the heat in the apartment bore down. Deena had never once seen her aunt cry. She was a tough, no-nonsense example of what it took to survive a Manhattan woman's life. Yet here she was with her face closing in on itself, eyes rimmed in red, cheeks wet with tears. The living room's four walls seemed to absorb the loss of Michael, turning the room into a memory box where Agatha's pain was destined to fester over time.

Deena brought her aunt a glass of water and then sat next to her, placing her hand on Agatha's knee. After a few sips Agatha grabbed a napkin, wiped her tears, and blotted the sweat from her upper lip and brow. She then rubbed her temples and with a deep sigh grabbed another cigarette, allowing the familiar hard edge in her eyes to return.

"Would you like to tell me what happened?" said Deena.

"Actually, no. But now that you mention it, I have something else I'd like to share. A piece of advice that will help you now that you've moved to New York."

She lit her cigarette, tilted back her head, and blew a stream of smoke into the air. Then, after pulling a shred of tobacco from the tip of her tongue, she served up a humorless smile and said, "Do it to them before they do it to you."

Agatha got up and headed to the kitchen. "We probably still have ice in the freezer. I'm having a vodka rocks. Want one?"

"Sure," said Deena, quietly.

Agatha brought back two ice-filled glasses, crossed to the bar, and poured a generous amount of vodka into each. "You know what occurs to me?" she said, handing Deena her drink. "I moved to New

York in '65, ready for a new life, just like you, and during my first week, there was a blackout." Agatha tapped a column of ash from her cigarette into the ashtray, took a drag and said, "What are the odds?"

9

Deena, Simon, and Morrie sat at Lincoln Ristorante, the new Lincoln Center darling, nursing their negronis as they waited for Jill to arrive. They were an unlikely trio: Morrie in his jeans and blazer; Simon wearing his usual khaki pants, sports jacket, and red tie; and Deena in a floral metallic jacket, hair swept into a messy bun, a pair of fuchsia glasses by her side.

"I love this place," said Deena, looking around the modern Italian restaurant with a smile. The floor-to-ceiling windows looked out on a massive Henry Moore sculpture in Lincoln Center Plaza. Even better, it was a stone's throw from the Vivian Beaumont, where they were the proud holders of tickets to the hottest show in town.

She eyed the various trays going past, trying to divine which dish from the menu she was seeing. They were all carefully composed on simple white plates—beautiful and sculptural. Defacing them seemed wrong. The waiters placed these works of art in front of diners with a flourish and just a little regret, as if to say, "Eat if you must."

"Jill certainly knows how to pick 'em," said Deena.

"Of course she does," said Morrie, smoothing his salt-and-pepper hair. "She's a food and beverage analyst. It's her job to keep up with the latest and greatest."

Simon laughed. "C'mon, Morrie. Jill is more hedonist than analyst. She just loves food."

"I take exception to that, my friend," shot back Morrie with mock anger. "My wife is a brilliant, dedicated businesswoman who keeps her finger on the pulse of Manhattan for purely professional reasons."

"Yeah, right," said Simon. "If you'd known her back in our Goldman days, you'd have a very different picture of the lovely Jill."

"Did I hear my name?"

They all turned toward Jill, who had just reached their table. She looked younger than her fifty-nine years, with her hair stylishly short, wearing an Hermès dress and Louboutin shoes.

"Dumpling." Morrie shot up and gave Jill a kiss. "I've been valiantly defending your honor."

"So what's the deal?" she said, settling into her seat. "Talking behind my back?"

"Well, Jelly old girl, Simon here is suggesting that after three years of marriage I don't know my own wife. He has the audacity to portray you as a lover of gluttony just because of a few late-night frivolities back at Goldman."

Jill laughed. "Can't deny we managed an intoxicated night or two as young analysts-in-crime."

"Those were the days," said Simon as he took Deena's hand. "Right, hon?"

"Do you ever miss it?" said Morrie. "I mean the galas. The parties. It must have been quite a ride."

"Nah. I love teaching my high school hoodlums. It's right where I belong."

"You've got to tell Morrie how you met," said Jill.

Deena and Simon looked at each other, smiling, and Simon said, "How about if you take this one?"

"Sure." Deena looked at Morrie and dramatically cleared her throat. "It was a grimy bar on St. Mark's Place down in the East Village. I'd waded through the sawdust, inhaled the accumulated nineteenth-century dirt—no charge, of course—and found myself a spot at the bar, when in walks Prince Charming."

"And what creative pickup line did the boy use?" asked Morrie.

Deena laughed. "As if."

"Intriguing," said Morrie.

"I was trying to get the bartender's attention when I noticed Simon sidling over to me—part of the slumming-it brigade of suited-and-tied office worker tourists. He was sneaking a peek in my direction, acting all suave and subtle."

"I was the definition of suave and subtle," said Simon, defending himself. "If you'd waited, I would have made the move of the century."

"If I'd waited, we'd still be standing there. So I turned to him and said, 'Do you wanna hear a story or tell a story?' "

"What?" said Morrie.

"Works every time," she said, "and on so many levels."

"Let me guess," said Morrie. "Our boy chose to hear a story."

"Bingo."

Morrie turned to Simon and said, "It must have been one helluva tale."

"As I recall," said Simon, "it had something to do with her pet squirrel dipping French fries into ketchup."

Morrie threw back his head and laughed.

"What's so funny?" said Deena. "It could've been true. Besides, I was trying to suss him out. A shared sense of humor is essential."

"He obviously passed the test or you wouldn't be sitting here."

Simon leaned back in his chair. "Let's just say Deena is a lucky, lucky girl."

Deena whipped her head in his direction. "Hah!"

Before Simon could manage a comeback, Jill spotted the waiter and said, "We'd better order."

After the server brought their meals, Jill gave Morrie a sideways look. "Well, are you going to tell her?"

"Tell me what?" asked Deena.

"Jelly, you're reading my mind." Morrie winked and turned to Deena. "You've heard of Carter Wilton, I presume?"

"Vat you tink, I come from village?" shot back Deena in her best Syrian accent.

"He's doing a staged reading of his newest play, *Call to the Faithful*—working out the kinks."

"So?"

"So . . ." said Morrie. "I had a fascinating conversation with his girlfriend, Brigitte Harper."

Jill interrupted. "Morrie sold her a co-op down in SoHo."

"Look at you, Morrie," said Deena. "Broker to the stars."

"That's me. A step from greatness." Morrie scanned everyone at the table. "So why, you may ask, would I share this tidbit?"

"Why, indeed," said Deena.

"Because, my love . . . I've arranged an audition for you with the casting director. There's a part in the show with your name on it."

"An audition?" Deena put down her wineglass mid-sip and leaned forward. "How did you pull *that* off?"

"I'm just that good, my dear."

Deena glanced at Simon, who was wearing one of his wide smiles. "Did you know about this?"

"Guilty." Then, reaching for her hand, he said, "There's no pressure, darling. You should only go if you feel up to it."

"Here's the thing," said Morrie. "I sent them excerpts of that production you did at the Roundabout—*Time for Tea*. They loved what they saw. While they're not hiring you sight unseen, you won't be going in cold. You just need to wait until they get back from Williamsburg."

"You're in the wrong business, Morrie," said Deena. "I bet you'd give my agent a run for his money."

"I don't know about that," laughed Morrie. "I've heard some impressive stories about the great Earl Aronson."

All true. And Deena was lucky to have him. Earl had stuck by her during her tough years and was now tiptoeing her into small regional auditions. She couldn't wait to tell him the news. Maybe this was her next step: a staged reading. A week's worth of rehearsals, tops. No costumes, no props . . . no pressure. At least, not much. She may even get cast when the play goes up. "I don't know what to say."

Morrie grinned, and interpreting the tears in her eyes as a yes, proclaimed, "When speechless, there is but one option." He picked up his wineglass. "A toast!"

———

They arrived at the Vivian Beaumont, fed, wined, and happy, just in time for the start of the show. Deena felt a rush of excitement as they were shown to their seats. Center orchestra. Leave it to Jill.

Once settled, she had that familiar sense of anticipation as they faced the closed curtain. Any minute now it would rise in a ta-da moment—like a mother playing a jumbo game of peekaboo. The pre-curtain chatter in the house blended each person's voice into a single distinctive drone. There wasn't another sound in the world like it.

The house lights finally went down and the curtain rose. With a minimal set, projections, and lighting, Act I was the embodiment of every 1940s film set in the English countryside with its thatched roofs and rural tranquility. But the scenery, the lighting, the projections—they were all secondary. It was the horses. My God. The horses overshadowed everything—life-size beasts able to be mounted and ridden. Three puppeteers were in control of every movement right down to the twitching of an ear. But to call it puppetry was like calling Buckingham Palace a pied-à-terre. These horses were living, breathing beings.

By the end of Act I, Deena was so breathless from the creativity of it she had to remind herself to breathe. The audience seemed bound together by what they'd seen and felt, yes—and also by what was next. Deena had read reviews about Act II, the battles, the lighting, the soundtrack. She couldn't wait.

The happy quartet headed to the bar for a quick drink, joking and laughing. The room was crowded with excited people. Energy was high.

And then Deena's phone rang.

"Don't answer," said Simon quickly. "Whoever it is will call back."

Deena heard his advice too late, not that she would have listened. It was Wilshire. In the month that Agatha had been there, they'd never once called. Simon was just going to have to deal with it.

"Mrs. Bartlett?" said a voice on the other end. "It's Susan Elliot from Wilshire Rehab. I'm sorry to disturb you, but your aunt has taken a turn for the worse."

And at that moment all the energy, all the joy in the room, collapsed into a void, leaving Deena standing alone, isolated, with the phone in her hand.

"How bad is it?"

"She's having tremendous difficulty breathing and . . . she's calling your name."

Deena knew she should say something but she couldn't find the words.

"Hello? Mrs. Bartlett? Are you there?"

"Yes . . . yes, I'm here," mumbled Deena mechanically. "I'm out of town at the moment but I'll be there as quickly as I can. Thank you for calling."

As she ended the call, Simon said, "Sweetheart, I'm sorry. We'll leave right after the show."

"No, Simon. There isn't a chance in hell I'm staying." She jammed her phone into her bag. "We need to leave. Now."

———

They said their good-byes and left for Grand Central. It was a grim trip back to Stanhope. As the train headed upstate, Deena stared at her reflection. The starless sky pressed against the window, pushing to get through, but the garish lighting inside the car wouldn't let it in. Deena wished it would. The night would have cushioned her, protected her from her thoughts. Was she angry? Resentful? Damn right. Even in her last moments on Earth, Agatha couldn't resist invoking a final flourish of selfish disruption.

What a terrible thing to think. The woman is dying and I resent the timing? Deena knew she was being shallow and heartless. The business of death was never convenient. Besides. Agatha didn't even know she was at the theater.

They arrived at eleven p.m. Agatha had a high fever, tearing at her nightgown, all while still asleep. Every time the nurse covered her with a sheet, she managed to throw it off. When it became clear that keeping Agatha covered was a losing battle, Simon looked at Deena and said, "It's okay with me if she's naked, so long as it doesn't bother you."

Deena nodded gratefully and the nurse let Agatha pull her sheet away until she lay fully exposed with the discarded sheet crumpled on the floor. Deena and Simon sat in chairs on either side of her and waited. Every once in a while, Agatha would let out a quiet moan.

Simon eventually fell asleep slumped in his chair, but Deena remained awake. She watched her aunt's small, round body, the breasts flattened and draped loosely on either side of her chest—face bloated, red blotches on both cheeks, breathing labored. The past forty years played through her mind: that first weekend in New York, their trips to the theater, the restaurants. Agatha wasn't an easy woman, but Deena was glad she'd stuck by her.

It was just past 4:30 in the morning when Agatha stirred. Deena sat at attention as a gravelly sound came from her aunt's lips. In a barely audible voice, Agatha said, "Deena."

Deena stood and moved closer. "I'm here, Aunt Agatha."

Her aunt smiled weakly and then, with great difficulty, said, "I've …"

"Yes, Aunt Agatha. I hear you."

"I've …"

Deena looked down at her ashen face.

"I've … got you now."

10

Deena's knees gave way as she nearly sank to the floor. She quickly grabbed the rail of the hospital bed for support. Her aunt couldn't have repeated those words from Brixton Playhouse because those words had never been spoken. They weren't real.

I won't allow this to happen. I'm stronger than this.

But, dammit ... maybe Simon *was* right. Maybe she had stretched herself so thin that the panic attacks she'd thought were gone had grown into something more. Hearing voices was a whole different ball game. Hearing voices meant she was losing her grip.

Deena needed to leave the room. There wasn't enough air.

She went out into the nearly deserted hallway and took the elevator down to the first floor. Then she walked through the revolving doors and stood outside breathing in the five a.m. gloom, with the glow from the Center's lobby at her back and a world of darkness ahead. The air was laden with a summer storm ready to give way, thick and still and sullen.

Deena stepped out from under the overhang and raised her face to the pinpricks of mist tingling against her forehead and cheeks.

The surrounding shadows protected her—the night, impenetrable except for a gash of predawn light balancing on the horizon, ripping heaven from earth. What was beyond that rift? She wished she could grab onto its edge, hoist herself up, and crawl into the opening. She imagined coming through on the other side into a world bathed in light, where she could lay herself down and allow the sun's warmth to gather her up in its arms.

Deena felt her shoulders release as her few minutes alone brought everything into perspective. It came down to this. Fatigue does crazy things to a person's mind. She had to hold on to that thought, because the alternative terrified her.

Enough. It was time to go back upstairs. These were Agatha's final hours, maybe even minutes. After everything they'd been through, Deena wasn't abandoning her now. She bolstered herself and went back up to the second floor. When she got to the room, Simon was just waking up.

"Damn," he said, standing to stretch. "I'm getting too old to sleep in a chair. My back is screaming." He glanced at Deena. "Hey, are you all right?"

She rubbed the back of her neck and stared out the window. "I didn't sleep much. Just tired."

Simon came up behind her and gave her a squeeze, binding them together with a ribbon of his cologne that brought with it a reminder of their night in the city. Had it really happened? Deena suddenly wanted to grab Simon, run home, pack their bags, and take the next train to New York. She wanted to turn her back on all of it—doubts about her sanity, her aunt, the rehab center . . . everything. In the city they'd resurrect their old life, a time when they held their future close to their breasts like a shiny new penny.

There was a sound at the door. It was the doctor.

"Morning," he said. "I understand you had quite a night. Let's take a look."

He went to the laptop sitting on its rolling cart next to Agatha's bed and checked the screen. "Hmm . . . How about that." The doctor walked toward Agatha. "Your aunt is looking . . . good. Her fever has broken, breathing steady. Heart rate in the realm of normal." He raised his eyebrows and added, almost to himself, "That is really something."

The doctor took off his glasses and turned to Deena. "If you want to go home, I'd say she's out of danger."

"I don't understand," said Simon. "Agatha has chosen comfort care. No medication. Are you saying her sepsis has just . . . disappeared? By itself?"

"It's rare, but not unheard of. She must be a real fighter. We'll see how she does over the next few days, but for now, Agatha is definitely doing better."

Deena felt the ground give way.

Better.

She sank into herself.

Of course she's better.

Sinking.

And it's no surprise.

Down. Down.

No surprise at all.

"Sweetheart," said Simon, gently, "let's go home." He led her, like a sleepwalker, from the room. When they reached the elevator they saw the cleaning lady, Jadwiga, standing in the shadows, staring at them as they passed.

———

When they got home they headed to bed. As for the concern on Simon's face, Deena chose to ignore it. She pulled the sheet over her clothes and pretended to fall asleep. After a couple of hours she heard him leave for work. It was a relief.

Telling Simon about the voices she'd been hearing was not going to happen. He'd grab onto it with both hands and drive her straight to the doctor. There would be no passing GO, no collecting two hundred dollars.

If only she could understand what was touching it off. She felt isolated and alone—except for the disturbing illusion of a single sentence whispered in a darkened theater, lying next to her as bedmate.

She was just about asleep when a scream startled her awake. Deena bolted upright with her breathing coming in fast, shallow bursts—until a vision across from her bed stopped that breathing in its tracks.

The opposite wall was gone, replaced by a dark house overgrown with brambles. Two large oak trees grew on either side, their shadows deepening the house's gloom. The smell of White Shoulders floated toward the bed. There, in the third-floor window, was her mother, looking out at Deena. She seemed . . . not angry. Worried was more like it. She was trying to say something, but Deena couldn't make out her words. It must have been important, because Zahra's hands were balled into fists and her head was craned forward.

Deena tried to get out of bed, but her legs wouldn't move.

What the hell's happening to me?

The familiar beginnings of a panic attack took over . . . the trembling in her hands, the pressure in her head. She focused on her breathing in an effort to gain control. She'd just about managed when she sensed the air collapsing in on itself.

The sound from Brixton Playhouse entered the room like an approaching train, slowly at first, then gathering speed. But the taunting laughter wasn't taunting anymore. It was maniacal, growing louder as it entered her head. This was unfinished business. It had been interrupted at Brixton, and somehow Deena knew it was angry. It wanted to hurt her, to scare her until all reason had been stripped away.

The laughter bounced against the sides of her skull, came out from her eyes, rolled around her tongue, vibrated through her hair. Deena screamed from the pain of it as she felt herself falling, falling, falling into a deep, dark hole.

Then a different sound joined in. Not a scream or a squeal or a laugh. It was a song Deena remembered from when she was young. And even though it was sung quietly, it rode above the cacophony, lilting and rocking. With each note, the laughter inside her head peeled away and fell to the floor until all that was left were the blessed strains of the long-ago melody.

She sat panting, her face, neck, and chest slick with sweat. When she looked up she caught sight of a movement from the third-floor window of the imagined house. Her mother was holding a baby—and Deena knew exactly who it was.

It was her. It was Deena.

Zahra brought her face close to the baby's cheek and kissed it as she hummed the Syrian lullaby Deena had heard more times than she could remember. Her mother rocked the baby back and forth, back and forth, until it dropped off to sleep. She then turned her face up to Deena and smiled.

Deena's grief was so deep and so wide that her throat swelled from the size of it. She wanted to lie next to her mother one more time. She wanted to talk about all she had missed. She wanted to reverse time and share a cup of coffee and laugh about this or that. She wanted to thank her for the rescue.

And she wanted to say, *I'm sorry.*

Then, as quickly as she had appeared, Zahra was gone.

11

The next morning, Deena felt as if her head was made of stone. If only she could separate her mind from her body. Then she could stay asleep a few hours longer while her body acted as proxy, going about its business, with no one the wiser.

The memory of last night's hallucination slowly filtered back into her mind. Because that was what it was. A hallucination.

What should I do? she thought, with her despair weighing her down.

Deena's crying came in deep, rasping gulps. What a fool, to think she was strong enough to weather this past year. The frightened teenager she thought she'd left behind had been waiting just below the surface for the perfect moment to take over. She had no choice but to enlist Simon's help, no matter how humiliated it made her feel. But she could at least ask him calmly. She just needed a little time for her fear to dissipate—to go about her business in the concrete, three-dimensional world. Then tonight, when Simon got home, they would talk.

She dragged herself out of bed and got ready for Wilshire. Home to Wilshire to home to Wilshire. The wheel kept turnin' round. But as she was walking out to the car, her phone rang.

"Oh my God, Deena," said an excited voice on the other end of the line. "Simon just told me the news."

It was Fiona. Loud, nosy, opinionated . . . and totally normal. Thank God she'd called.

"Let me guess," said Deena. "The audition, right?"

"Yes! And shame on you for not calling me. That's no way to treat a friend."

"God, Fiona, it only happened last night. You were the first call on my list."

"Hmmph. Okay. I'll buy that. But we have important business to discuss. What will you be wearing?"

The thought of a dress was the last thing on Deena's mind, but she had to admit that it was firmly in the "concrete, three-dimensional world".

"Actually," said Deena, "I don't have a clue."

"Good. Because I'm dying to go shopping. Besides, you owe me lunch. I don't take kindly to welchers."

Deena did owe Fiona lunch. More than one, in fact. Fiona had been with her every step of the way after Agatha's apartment fire. It wasn't just the casseroles she dropped off. There'd been a particularly divert-ing gin-themed lunch when Deena had been desperate for a break.

"If it's lunch you want," said Deena, "it's lunch you'll get. Next week?"

"Perfect. But you're not getting off that easy. I also need to dish on what happened. Whaddya say? Java Joe's? Ten o'clock?"

Deena offered up her best approximation of a laugh. "Yes, Fiona— Java Joe's, ten o'clock."

Everybody in town went to Java Joe's, Stanhope's ersatz community center, and at ten o'clock Wednesday morning the place was packed. Deena scanned the crowded room and spotted Fiona sitting in the back. When she got to the table, Fiona stood at her full five-foot-ten height and gave Deena a hug.

"I've ordered you a cappuccino," she said, combing her fingers through her spiky red hair. "Now, tell—wait, are you okay?"

Damn it. Deena had hoped she could hide the worry tugging at the corners of her eyes, but fooling Fiona had never been easy. She had no choice but to deflect.

"Just tired," she said, and then launched into what had happened with Morrie. She rambled on about his connection to Carter Wilton's girlfriend, his surprise news—all of it. And it worked. Fiona was swept into the story and quickly forgot the dark clouds behind Deena's eyes.

With a shared bagel between them Fiona said, "We should go to the city for our shopping trip. And don't think for a second that throwing a bagel down my throat counts as reciprocation. We'll have lunch before we shop. Odeon would be fun. We can pretend to be tourists."

"I don't know, Fiona. Going to the city would take all day. My aunt—"

"God, Deena, stop. This audition is important."

Deena looked at her watch, feeling a pull to leave. "Fine. Next Wednesday works."

"Great!" Fiona stared at Deena for a second, her face suddenly serious. "What gives? Every time you talk about Agatha your shoulders end up around your ears."

"I owe her."

"Seems to me she's the one who owes you."

"Not back in the day. She got me my start as an actor."

"Agatha was an actor?"

Deena gave a little laugh at the thought. "No. Aunt Agatha was the business manager at Manheim Theater Group. But it goes deeper than that. For one thing, we're connected."

"Families usually are."

"No. I mean *really* connected. In a strange way."

"I don't follow."

In the three years that Deena had known Fiona, she'd never thought to share these stories, just as she'd never shared much about her years acting in New York. She looked at Fiona's puzzled face and thought, *Why not?*

"Well, for instance," she began, "we were born exactly twenty years apart, to the day. And believe it or not, on both nights there was a storm." Deena laughed. "Simon calls this dinner party banter, but it's true."

"Okay," said Fiona, "I'll bite. What else?"

"Little things. Meaningless, really, but when you put them all together . . . like I said, strange."

"You're being way too coy for comfort. I want to hear everything."

"Okay, here's another example. At twelve I broke my left ankle when my bike rolled over an old shoe. Aunt Agatha broke her left ankle at the same age when her bike ran over a rock."

"Hmmph," said Fiona. "That's . . . a coincidence."

"Then there was my first apartment in New York. Turns out it was directly across the hall from my aunt's first apartment."

"All right. Now we've crossed over. Connected."

"There's more. Besides being connected, Aunt Agatha and I grew close after my parents died. We even went on vacation together."

"You gotta be kidding. Where?"

Deena smiled at the memory. "A week in London. It was 1979, a couple of months after my father's funeral. I'd been living in New

York for two years with an acting résumé that amounted to serving burgers at O'Neal's Baloon to the after-theater crowd. Aunt Agatha figured a week in London would do me good."

"And did it?"

"Oh, God, yes. There's nothing like theater in London, particularly when you go with someone like my aunt. She knew everybody. I got a chance to go backstage at some tremendous productions."

"I thought she was tough. Unapproachable."

"When I was a kid she was way more than unapproachable. She couldn't stand the sight of me. Actually, she can't stand the sight of me now. Our middle years, however, were a different story. We got along great. Until Simon came into the picture. That's when everything fell apart."

"Why?"

"No idea."

After a bit more small talk, they settled on the following Wednesday for their trip to the city. It was tempting to order another bagel for no other reason than to put off leaving, but no. It was time to get to Wilshire.

———

When Deena arrived at the rehab center, the heaviness of the place erased whatever respite she'd felt with Fiona. It was that damn hallucination last night, walking beside her, whispering in her ear. Fiona's happy chattering had chased it away for a while, but now, murmurs and sighs seemed to come from every open door she passed.

When she got to Agatha's room, the privacy curtain was drawn. She could hear there was a nurse with her aunt, so she decided to poke her head into Maggie Doherty's room. That should make her feel better.

"Why, Deena, how nice to see you. Come in."

"Hi, Maggie. How's it going?"

"Couldn't be better. *Ma tête* is feeling clearer every day. And your aunt?"

"It was a rough night, but she made it through."

"Well, if you don't mind my saying, it looks like you had a rough night as well. Are you all right?"

Deena felt herself tearing up.

"You poor, sweet thing," said Maggie. "Come in and tell me everything."

Deena sat next to Maggie's bed and took out a tissue. "I'll be fine," she said, blotting the corner of her eye. "I didn't get much sleep last night."

Maggie sat up in bed a little straighter. "I've watched how wonderful you are with your aunt, but anyone can see that you need a break." She leaned in closer to Deena. "Here's a thought. If she wakes up to an empty room, I would be happy to sit with her until you arrive."

"Believe me, you don't want to do that. She can be difficult."

"I don't mind," said Maggie. "When you're as old as we are, you're bound to get short-tempered from time to time. As I say to my children, 'Getting old would be easier if we were young while we were doing it.'"

Deena felt herself loosen up. *I love this woman.* Maybe she had finally found what she'd been missing all these years. Someone like her mother to lean on.

"That would be a big help, Maggie. Thank you." Deena glanced at the clock on the wall. "I suspect they're finished with Aunt Agatha by now. I'd better go check on her. But it's been great visiting."

"It's wonderful to see you too, my dear. Good luck with your aunt."

Deena gave a wave and went next door just as the privacy curtain around Agatha's bed was being drawn back. There she was, sitting up, wide awake, staring . . . at absolutely nothing. And if the crinkles around her eyes and her slightly upturned mouth was any indication, it was making Agatha very, very happy.

A shiver rolled over Deena's shoulders. She quickly shrugged it off and pulled up a chair. But when she reached for Agatha's hand, her aunt didn't turn her head, didn't make a sound—didn't even notice she was there.

Deena sat there for an hour trying to concentrate on her book, but her aunt's unbroken trance was unsettling.

When the doctor came by doing rounds, he checked the monitor and then placed his hand on Agatha's shoulder.

"Hello, Ms. Haddad. It's Dr. Montero. How are you feeling today?"

There was no response—not even acknowledgment that someone was speaking.

Dr. Montero listened to her heart and checked her breathing.

"So what do you think, Doctor?" asked Deena. "Will she get better?"

He motioned Deena out to the hall. Once there, he lowered his head and gave her a hard stare.

"Mrs. Bartlett, I'll be surprised if your aunt lasts another week. As to her current stabilization, these things sometimes happen, but it would be a mistake to get your hopes up. At the risk of sounding harsh, you need to come to terms with her passing."

And to Deena's surprise—and not a little shame—she felt the promise of a new day.

12

After the doctor left, Deena sat by a silent, unmoving Agatha for another hour. Deena's head lolled and her mouth relaxed as she nodded off into a half-sleep. Every once in a while she roused herself, but as quickly as she found consciousness she drifted away again. The cycle was finally broken by a quiet chuckle coming from the bed, snapping Deena awake.

Agatha's head was turned in her direction, her eyes wide open and her mouth formed into a toothy grin. She was laughing—and there was nothing happy about it.

Deena shot up from her chair and backed up toward the door as Agatha lowered her head, all the while holding Deena with her stare. Her aunt's laugh was low and quiet and cruel. A tiny drop of spittle clung to the corner of her mouth as she whispered, "Deeeenahhh."

Deena felt the blood drain from her face. Then a voice from behind said, "Are you all right, Mrs. Bartlett?"

She swung around to see one of the young nurses standing in the doorway.

"Yes, thank you," she stammered. "It's my aunt. She's awake and—"
But when she turned back around Agatha was sound asleep.

The nurse stared at Deena with concern. "You look tired. Why don't you go home and get some rest? We'll take it from here."

Oh, God. Another hallucination. It was getting worse. If there was any part of her that doubted she should tell Simon, it was now gone.

Deena mumbled a good-bye and bolted from the room with her fear clinging to her like a bad dream. Simon would be home from school by now. She needed to put aside her pride and tell him what had been happening. It was time to face the humiliating fact that she needed help—that she was a sick, sick woman.

It was a miserable ride home. Deena kept seeing her aunt's face staring at her. The menace in her eyes. The wide grin. The echo of her laugh. That horrible, horrible laugh. The longer she drove, the tighter her hands clutched the steering wheel—as if holding onto it would stop her from falling off the edge of the Earth.

She quickly parked the car and, thank God, Simon was home. She hurried to the front door, rehearsing what she'd say. She would be honest. It was time to get help.

But when Deena stepped inside she could hear a disturbing conversation going on in the kitchen. Simon was on the phone, and he was talking about her.

"I *am* worried, Claire," he said. "She was a zombie last night."

It was his perfect sister. The condescending way Claire had treated Deena when she was in therapy still stuck in Deena's craw. She quietly stationed herself in the hall by the kitchen to listen.

"No, it's not my imagination," he said. "I think Deena is primed for a relapse . . . That's a kind offer, but you know Deena . . . Let me think on it. She's very fragile . . . Yup . . . Okay. I'll let you know. And Claire, thanks for checking on us."

How dare he! thought Deena. How dare he bring his sister into this. If Simon was all that concerned he could damn well do more than criticize. Where was he when she'd been dealing with the fire? Everything had fallen on her shoulders. But what was really putting her into orbit was that he said she was fragile. How was she supposed to share what was going on when he went around telling people she was on the verge of some kind of collapse?

Then it hit her. He must have talked to Morrie and Jill. That was why Morrie had set up the Carter Wilton audition. And there was no way two extra tickets to *War Horse* had just magically materialized. Jill must have spent a fortune. The more Deena thought about it, the angrier she got.

She dropped her keys on the vestibule table.

"Deena? Is that you?" called Simon.

"I'm home. Just going up to change."

Ten minutes later she walked into the kitchen as Simon was pulling a couple of steaks from the refrigerator.

"I hope you're hungry," he said, "because these rib eyes look mighty fine." He turned around for a kiss and then stopped short. "What is it? What's the matter?"

Deena headed to the liquor cabinet and poured herself a scotch.

"Deena, I said, what's the matter?"

"Well," said Deena, as she took a healthy sip from her glass, "you tell me—because it would appear I am too fragile to grasp the full extent of what's going on."

Simon blanched. "You heard me talking to Claire."

Deena slammed her drink onto the table. "You're damn right I heard you talking to Claire. Jesus, Simon, how could you?"

"Sweetheart, listen." Simon moved over to Deena and tried to put his arms around her, but she pushed him away. "For God's sake, Deena, listen to me for a second."

Deena turned her back and stared out the window, trying to regain her composure.

"Look at yourself," he said. "I know it's tough, but you're being eaten alive. The way you looked last night when we came home from

Wilshire worried the hell out of me. You could barely put one foot in front of the other. Just the fact that you're this upset about my conversation with Claire says it all. Your aunt has worn you down. She's eroded everything you are. Agatha has—"

"Agatha! Agatha! Agatha! I can't stand hearing that name." Deena swung around with her anger taking the lead. "Y'know what? I'm going to stop thinking about Aunt Agatha and get my life back. Me. By myself. I don't need you *or* your family's pity!"

"*My* family? It's our family. Claire loves you."

"Oh, please. I hear the tone she uses on me. That 'poor-Deena' smile. I would never accept help from your sister. How does it feel, Simon, to come from a perfect family? You and your sister and your parents are straight out of a Norman Rockwell painting. The New England Bartletts—perfect in every way."

"What the hell are you saying?"

"I'm saying that for years I've been poor little orphan Deena, saddled with a demanding aunt. When I'm around your family I feel like a beggar. Everything I come from, everything I am, is minimized by the sainted Bartletts."

"Are you saying I don't appreciate where you come from?"

"Well? Do you?"

"I can't believe what I'm hearing. I wouldn't be married to you if I didn't love everything you are. Think, Deena. We've been together for twenty-five years."

"Okay, fine. You love everything I am, everything I come from. Including my aunt."

"You can't be serious."

"You bet I'm serious."

Simon stared at Deena for a moment, the muscles in his jaw flexing as he closed his eyes and let out a frustrated breath. "You should see the look on your face when Agatha is around. The way you hold your body. Even *you* hate being with her."

"No, I don't. I owe her everything."

"Bullshit. Your aunt has spent years grinding you into the ground. Not only that, she's done everything in her power to drive a wedge between us. I don't know what I did, I don't know what I said, but she has hated me from the day we met. If she'd had her way, you'd be living a single life, focused on her and only her."

Deena quietly turned her back and looked out the window. She didn't answer because everything Simon said was true. The day she'd introduced Simon to her aunt was the day a battle royale had begun. And for twenty-five years, all Deena could do was stay out of the way.

13

1987

Deena looked at herself in the mirror. *That should do it.* She was a mishmash of layers and colors. Short skirt, ankle-high hiking boots, and beads—tons of beads. She rolled the sleeves of her bomber jacket up past her elbows. The shoulder pads made her look even thinner than she was. Then she fluffed her mane of curls and gave her makeup a once-over. Simon would be there any minute, and she wanted to look her best.

Things were moving fast. For the past two months they'd spent most of their time together. Was it too soon to imagine Simon was *the one?* Deena didn't care how soon it was. She knew how she felt.

The buzzer rang and she went to the intercom. "Hello?"

"It's me."

Deena buzzed Simon up, and in a few seconds he was knocking at her door.

"You're here early," she said.

Simon stepped into her fourth-floor walk-up, more closet than apartment. There was a broken-down couch along one wall that Deena had grabbed at the Salvation Army on 46th Street. It may have been only six blocks from her apartment, but getting that monster down the street, to her building, and up the stairs took the promise of three pizzas and a case of beer. It sat proudly across from one of Deena's trash finds, a nearly perfect rattan armchair. Actually, most of the apartment was furnished courtesy of her favorite store—the trash piles of New York.

Simon grabbed Deena by the waist and planted a big kiss on her just-made-up face.

"Your neighborhood is up to form," he joked. "There was some guy at Fifty-second and Tenth happy to sell me any flavor of pills that struck my fancy. I guess that's why they call it Hell's Kitchen. Get it? Hell's *Kitchen?*"

"There you go again, teasing me about where I live." She took his face in both hands and came in, nose to nose. "Not everybody can afford an apartment at Sixty-ninth and Third." Then she gave him a kiss and turned to get her handbag.

"You should work someplace more upscale. The waitresses at Anabelle's are probably making a fortune."

"I'd never leave O'Neal's Baloon," she said, checking her reflection one more time. "There's nothing better than working side by side with a bunch of theater gypsies. I'm right where I belong."

Simon looked at Deena with a wide grin. "And *that's* what makes you great." He grabbed her again, twirled her toward him, and started kissing her in earnest.

"Mmm. Simon. Wait. We've gotta get to Aunt Agatha's."

Simon pulled away with a grimace. "After everything you've told me, I'm a little scared."

Deena laughed, snatched up her bag, and said, "Let's go."

They headed to the Port Authority subway station, passing occasional homeboys carrying monster boom boxes on their shoulders, their full-throttled music used as a force field to protect them from enemy combatants. After a ten-minute wait on the A, C, E platform they boarded a graffiti'd A train headed downtown.

Deena had to admit she was a little nervous about their visit. Agatha could be unpredictable with people she didn't know, but she was all the family she had. It was important her aunt like Simon.

"I know I've told you crazy stories about my aunt, but I owe her a lot. Keep in mind that these past few years have been rough. I never knew the particulars about her breakup with Michael, but after he was gone she threw herself with intent into a sea of men."

"That breakup was a long time ago. I'm surprised she hasn't found someone new."

"She's tried. Since Michael, Aunt Agatha has become a player, dating anybody and everybody. And by 'dating,' I mean in the biblical sense. Sometimes she even double-books—one man in the afternoon, a quick change of sheets, and a second man at night. Problem is, they're usually married. It's not that she *wants* to be with married men, but the few times she's met someone single, fate has conspired against her."

"How?"

"Take Andrei. He was arrested as a Russian spy and sent to Leavenworth."

"Oh c'mon, Deena."

"It's true! I have the newspaper article to prove it. And that's just the beginning. There was Sidney, who was killed in the lobby of the Chase Manhattan Bank by a panicked bank robber. Then Artie, who got amnesia after being hit on the head with a flower pot from a third-floor window."

Simon's eyes crinkled as he threw back his head and laughed. "Oh my God. You're too much."

"I'm serious! Bottom line, Aunt Agatha was meant to stay single. It has been written."

They emerged from the A train and after a short walk, reached Agatha's building off Washington Square.

"Wow," said Simon. "Some place."

The Brevoort on Fifth Avenue had a grand entrance with a circular drive set off by a landscaped patch in the center. The generous space was striking in a town like New York where most buildings were jammed together cheek by jowl.

"Wait till you see her apartment," said Deena. "She's so lucky. Aunt Agatha was living here before it went co-op—got in on the insider price."

"Damn. It's got to be worth plenty."

"Such a capitalist," laughed Deena.

"But I'm cute, right?" Simon grabbed her by the waist and squeezed.

They walked through the doors into a large, marble-floored lobby. Directly across from the entrance was a wall of glass through which they could see a beautiful inner garden planted with grass and flowers. After being announced they took the elevator to the fourteenth floor.

Agatha answered her door wearing a paisley caftan, holding a lit cigarette in her hand. At fifty-three she was a woman working hard to look young. Her dyed hair, too black, was styled just above her shoulders with severe bangs grazing her heavily plucked eyebrows.

"Hi, Aunt Agatha," said Deena giving her a hug.

"Come in, come in," said Agatha, eyeing Deena's outfit with obvious disapproval.

"Aunt Agatha, I'd like you to meet Simon. Simon, my aunt."

As they shook hands, Agatha took the measure of him with her eyes going from his hair to his clothes to his shoes. "How about a glass of red?" she said, turning to usher them into the living room.

"Sure."

She grabbed two wineglasses, nearly dropping one on the floor. It was her hands. Once beautiful, they were aging prematurely, not

79

that arthritis was the culprit. After years of pretentious posing, Agatha's hands had begun to atrophy. Her fingers were unaccustomed to bending more than the restricted graceful curve she had perfected.

Deena and Simon sat together on the couch with their legs touching one another's, as new lovers are wont to do. It was a comfortably sized room with simple modern furniture—burnt-orange cube chairs, gray tufted couch, clear Lucite coffee table, Persian rugs, all in beautiful taste.

Agatha handed them their wine and sat on the chair opposite the couch.

"I'm surprised at you, Deena," said Agatha with a smile, "keeping Simon under wraps for . . . how long? Two months? He's different from your usual starving-actor type." She turned to Simon. "What did you say your last name was, dear?"

"Bartlett."

"Ah, you're an Anglo."

Deena blanched and stole a look at Simon, who managed to keep his polite smile in place.

"What do you do?"

"I'm a pharmaceutical analyst at Goldman Sachs."

"Hmm," said Agatha. "Well, I've always believed that on the ladder of life the only thing lower than a doctor is a money changer. Seems to me you're a bit of both."

"Aunt Agatha!"

"Oh," said Agatha, turning to Deena. "Did I say something wrong?"

"It's all right, Deena," said Simon. "I admire honesty."

"You *admire honesty*," said Agatha, with an acid edge. "Very nice."

The rest of the visit was filled with pregnant silences and aborted attempts at finding common ground. Deena and Simon stayed for another hour and then invited Agatha to the Minetta Tavern for dinner. She declined—thank God.

As they rode down the elevator Deena said, "Oh, Simon, I don't know what got into her. I mean, she's not the easiest person in the world, but damn, that was terrible. I'm so sorry."

Simon smiled. "Call me crazy but . . . I don't think she likes me."

14

Deena's fight with Simon was a classic rendition of cutting off her nose to spite her face. It had stopped her from asking for the help she needed.

What had pushed her over the edge was the memory of Claire's exaggerated concern when Deena was in therapy—the way she left Deena out of anything substantive, as if Deena was, yes, yes, yes, too fragile to participate. Simon's conversation with his sister was tantamount to pressing his finger into an open wound. For God's sake, they'd been married for twenty-five years. He knew how she felt—how hard she'd worked to reinvent herself.

After a tense dinner they spent the rest of the night in different parts of the house. Simon got himself settled in his office and Deena made her way to the living room couch where she did her best to read the latest unreadable Samuel Baxter novel. But she was so jumpy the words on the page blended into an unrecognizable blur of ink. Shadows whispered in her ear, the windows followed her movements, hot breath blew against her cheek.

Stop.

Deena was desperate for relief. If fatigue had created this frame of mind, rest would surely turn her back into a normal, thinking woman. She resolved to spend less time at Wilshire. That should help. She would also focus on herself. Have some fun.

She was looking forward to going to the city with Fiona next week. It was the perfect place to start.

———

Fiona picked Deena up in a cab for their ride to the train station. She called it "planning ahead." This way, there would be no worries about drinking and driving on their trip back home.

Once on the train and settled in, Fiona said, "So, how are you doing? Really."

"Everything's good."

Fiona leaned back in her seat. "Jesus. After all this time you still pull the silent routine. If I wasn't a saint, I'd have dropped you years ago."

Deena turned toward the window and looked out at the Hudson River just as the train passed West Point with its turrets and stone walls. It seemed so solid and real and safe. She would give anything to be inside those walls, protected from whatever was happening. Deena was under siege and her own husband had joined in. With an edge to her voice she said, "Did Simon tell you to call me?"

"I know that tone, missy. Just what are you getting at?"

Deena shared the argument she and Simon had had last week. Then she pointedly looked at Fiona and said, "I can picture you being one of the people he'd call, sounding the fragile-Deena alarm."

Fiona poked Deena's shoulder with a little more force than necessary. "Get over yourself. He never said a word. If I can't have a day

83

with my friend without her worrying about ulterior motives, we don't need to do this."

Shit. Deena was blowing it with everybody. "Sorry, Fiona. To tell you the truth, it's been tough."

"Okay, let's start again. How are you doing?"

"I've been . . . imagining things." She quickly added, "Please don't tell Simon."

"What kinds of things?"

"Well, for one, my mother. I've sensed her a couple of times—which seems fine. But the other night I actually saw her. It felt so real."

"Believe me, I understand. And it's perfectly normal. After my mother died last year, I see her wherever I go."

Could that be it? thought Deena. "I don't know. *My* mother died thirty years ago."

"Okay, how about this?" Fiona did a quarter turn toward Deena, looked at her through lowered eyebrows, and said, "You sit in that goddamn rehab center for hours stewing over the past. Don't deny it: I know you. There's nothing like stewing over the past to bring it back to the present."

That made sense. Maybe Fiona was right.

"So here's Dr. Fiona's prescription for the miss-my-momma blues: a day of shopping and a boozy lunch."

Deena laughed. Nobody could accuse Fiona of deep thought. Her solution to *everything* was a day of shopping and a boozy lunch.

Their train groaned into the station and they walked up the steamy platform out to the main terminal. Deena never got tired of Grand Central. She looked up at the constellation of stars, laughing at the idea that the entire thing was reversed. As the story goes, when the artist copied the diagram for the ceiling, he placed it at his feet instead of holding it above his head. Hence, the reversal. The best part was that, after several renovations, the mistake had never been corrected.

In true Fiona fashion, they went to lunch first.

God, it was great to be downtown again. There was, of course, construction everywhere, but that's just how Manhattan rolled. When they walked past Deena's Tribeca apartment building, she wistfully said, "Sometimes I wish we'd never moved."

"C'mon. You had no choice. The exodus after 9/11 was like rats deserting a sinking ship." Fiona's eyebrows shot up. "Oops. Looks like I just called you a rat."

Deena laughed. "Fiona, I would expect nothing less."

Odeon hadn't changed. The food was okay—not great—but Fiona had chosen the place because it was one of Deena's old haunts. They were there for the memories. Not every restaurant gives you the chance to sit three tables away from Chris Farley, high to the bejeezus-belt.

They started off with a pair of Ricards (no ice, please, water on the side), and then moved to Niçoise salads with a bottle of Chenin Blanc. The world according to Fiona proclaimed that a bottle of wine was just right for two people.

Lunch was a much-needed blast. There's nothing like good food to lubricate the conversation.

Deena and Fiona had formed an instant connection after one of Brixton's opening nights three years ago—a horrible production of *Godspell*, of all things. But this was regional theater. Musicals sold tickets. Fiona had overheard Deena mumbling, "Thank God that's over," and let out a guffaw. Before long they were huddled in a quiet corner whispering ungenerous comments about the production, after which the four of them—Simon, Deena, Fiona, and her husband, Billy—went out for a drink, laughing together till the bar closed.

Fiona and Billy divorced two years later, giving her plenty of outrageous stories to share about her after-marriage Dating Game.

With the last of their baguettes dragged through the Niçoise dressing, Fiona lobbied for dessert at Serafina. They made the greatest profiteroles, and it was just a two-block walk. Twenty minutes later, they were tucked into a shared plate of deliciousness washed down with two glasses of Veuve. If they hadn't ordered the double espressos afterwards, they never would have made it out. This was clearly what Deena had needed. She was already feeling lighter.

After paying the tab, they planted themselves in front of the restaurant, looking for a cab to take them uptown. Every brick and stone was imbued with memories of her early years with Simon. The cabs, the storefronts, the noise, the smell. She loved it all.

Deena craned her head to look back at their old building.

"Geez, Fiona," she said, "it's exactly the way I left it." She turned to her friend for a hug, but then stopped as she felt the blood drain from her face.

Fiona's spiky red hair and Irish profile had been replaced by a mane of lush black hair falling down around her shoulders and the unmistakable complexion of a Middle Eastern woman.

Her mother. It was happening again.

At the sound of Deena's gasp, Zahra turned toward her and in a faraway voice said, "Deena, be careful."

No. Please, no. Deena felt herself swaying as disturbing images passed in front of her eyes. A knife carving into a woman's neck. A teacup swirling with an earthy brew. A pillow held over a struggling face. What did it all mean?

Her mother grabbed her elbow and in a louder, more insistent voice, said, "Deena! Be careful!"

But she was falling down, down. Vines broke through the pavement and wound around her legs, pulling her into a deep hole. She struggled to get free, but wasn't strong enough.

"Look at me!"

Zahra's voice startled Deena awake—but it was now Fiona who had her by the elbow. "I said, be careful! You're going to fall."

Deena was teetering on the edge of the curb, ready to tumble into the street. She raised her hand to her forehead and said, "Maybe I'd better sit down. We've had a lot to drink."

Fiona helped her back into Serafina, where they sat and caught their breath. The restaurant supplied a damp napkin for her forehead and a cold glass of water, but the way Fiona stared at her was pushing Deena even further over the edge. She had to get away from her friend's look of concern.

She escaped to the ladies' room and closed herself into a stall, jamming the back of her hand into her mouth to keep her convulsive sobs from being heard. Deena could deny it no longer. She had crossed over into the land of mental illness, facing years of therapy, maybe even institutionalization. Simon would sound the alarm to everyone they knew. She would never be able to show her face again.

The door opened and Fiona called, "How are you doing, Deena? Need any help?"

"I'll be out in a minute. If you could order me a cup of coffee, that would be great."

Once she heard Fiona leave, Deena came out from the stall. Maybe if she focused on her health, got into a routine, made sure to rest, she wouldn't have to go to Simon for help. She might just be able to stop this thing in its tracks. She could even go a step further. Anytime she saw or heard something that didn't make sense, she'd simply pretend it wasn't there. Because, for God's sake, it wasn't.

Deena checked her face in the mirror and, as she suspected, it was a disaster. She freshened her makeup and then walked out into the restaurant, where Fiona was waiting at the bar with her coffee.

"Would you mind if we headed home?" said Deena. "I think the alcohol has done me in."

Fiona tried to cover her concern, but her jaunty smile couldn't hide her eyebrows coming together in a worried line. "That's what happens when you let yourself get out of shape. I've got another prescription for you. No less than two scotches on an empty stomach every morning for a month."

Deena laughed weakly. "Yes, Doctor."

15

Two weeks passed. Deena now had a regimen that she was holding on to with a firm grip. She got up at seven a.m. and went for a run. Then she took a long shower, got dressed, and tidied the house. She arrived at Wilshire by eleven and was gone by three p.m. Those days of morning-to-night visits were a thing of the past. She ate healthy, kept the house neat. Had a proper dinner with Simon every night. Spent time with Fiona.

And through it all, she pretended that everything was fine.

As each day dropped into place, another layer grew over Deena's memory of what she'd been through. The incident at Serafina, that night after the theater, the hallucination in her bedroom, Brixton. It had all been buried under a protective layer of callused skin. And the plan was working. She hadn't had a single incident since that day in the city. Deena's new best friend was a well-ordered life.

It was a Thursday like any other. Deena got to Agatha's by eleven to find Maggie sitting next to her sleeping aunt. Her knitting needles click, click, clicked like a well-oiled factory machine as she looked up at Deena standing in the doorway.

"Why hello, dear."

Deena walked into the room and, seeing the label of Maggie's blouse sticking out from behind her neck, went round behind her and tucked it in.

Maggie laughed. "Oh my," she said. "I never was one for careful dressing."

"How are you today, Maggie?"

"Wonderful. Agatha and I had a lovely visit this morning before she dropped off to sleep. Poor thing has a hard time keeping her eyes open."

It flew in the face of reason that gentle Maggie had managed a relationship with her aunt. As Maggie told it, the first time they met, Agatha had launched a classic volley at Maggie's starboard side with a well-aimed "Who the hell are you?" Maggie dodged the salvo and parried with a smile and an introduction. Oddly enough, that was that.

End of case. Over and out. Done and dusted. Deena wished she'd been a fly on the wall.

"Oh my," said Maggie, glancing up at the wall clock. "I have to get to PT." She tucked her knitting into the basket by her side and lifted herself up off the chair. "Perhaps I'll see you later."

"Hope so."

Deena watched Maggie leave, wishing that some of her sweetness would rub off on Agatha. *As if,* she thought. That frightening vision of her aunt leering at her with an evil smile and an even more evil voice didn't come from nowhere. Years of suffering Agatha's jibes had clearly brought Deena to the edge.

But she was fine now. Just fine. She settled in, grateful that her aunt was asleep. Yet, even with that small mercy, the sounds of Wilshire took up whatever quiet was in the room. She had now memorized every annoying kink. The beeping, the nurses, the hushed voices, the crying patients: at first heart-wrenching; now so much white noise added to the soundscape. Deena checked the time. *Noon. Only noon.*

90

She had to leave at 1:30 for Kayla's first coaching and even though she'd only just arrived, time was crawling.

After another half hour, Agatha opened her eyes. It was strange to see her aunt without makeup, nails jagged, hair smashed flat from her pillow. Agatha loved throwing vicious jabs at anyone who didn't keep themselves well-groomed. She especially enjoyed giving Deena the once over. To see her lying in her current state gave Deena a guilty sense of exoneration.

Agatha looked at her with an angry squint and said, "Where's Maggie?"

"She's at PT. Do you need something?"

"What the hell do you think? I'm in pain, for Chrissake. Tell one of those damn nurses I need medication."

Ah, for those days of blessed silence. But if wishes were fishes we'd have some fried. Agatha may have beaten sepsis, but her COPD and heart condition were stepping into the batter's box, ready to hit it out of the park. There was no telling how long that would take. Forget about the doctor's one-week-left prediction. It was now three weeks since that interrupted evening in the city with her friends and Agatha's false alarm.

Deena wearily got the nurse. Then, after sharing lunch with her aunt ("The food here is revolting"), she left for Kayla's first coaching.

———

It was one of those summer days when the heat seemed to weigh the trees down. Deena's mind wandered as her Subaru pushed through the heavy air. The car was quickly becoming her sanctuary . . . a private place where she could go over her day. She was looking forward to Kayla's coaching, in part because it brought to mind her early years as an acting student.

Her mother never understood Deena's draw to acting but her father, oddly enough, did. Deena remembered the night she'd announced that she wanted to be an actor. Her father was the one who'd eased the tension in the air. After Zahra had gone to bed, Deena joined him in the living room.

"Why acting?" he'd asked in the light of the solitary lamp sitting on the table by his recliner.

Deena had stumbled through an incoherent explanation when her father, thankfully, interrupted. "Would it surprise you to learn that I wanted to be a sailor?"

"You mean, like, in the navy?"

"No," he laughed. "What I wanted more than anything was to work on a cruise ship doing any job they'd give me. The plan was to learn enough so that, some day, I could captain my own."

"So, how did you end up with a hardware store?"

"It was my father. He'd gotten sick and needed help at the shop. It was only supposed to be for a little while, but . . . well, you know how things go."

Deena loved thinking back on that night. The thing that stayed with her most was the way her father had peered over the rim of his coffee cup as he'd said, "You'll make a wonderful actress. Just make sure to get us good seats for your first show."

———

It was 1:45 when Deena got home for Kayla's 2:00 p.m. session. But she was met by a patched-up Ford Escort in her driveway, already parked and waiting.

Damn it, she thought. *They're here early.*

Deena got out of her car and hurried over to the Ford just as Kayla was stepping out onto the gravel driveway. Before Deena could introduce herself, Kayla's mother did a quick three-point turn and sped off, leaving Kayla standing like an abandoned calf clutching a notebook against her chest. Deena looked at her and thought, *If only she knew how beautiful she was.*

And beauty hardly described it.

Kayla was luminous, with the afternoon sun at her back, her skin impossibly pale, eyebrows and lashes barely visible, and astonishing blue eyes made all the more startling by the blue shirt she wore. Added to these gifts was her hair—coils the color of corn silk hanging loosely around her face, the light shining through the wisps, creating its own halo.

Deena was surprised by her surge of longing at the idea of a daughter—something she and Simon had decided against. She quickly tamped down the feeling. Having children wasn't for everyone. It sure as hell wasn't for her.

She gave Kayla a smile and said, "Good to see you. Ready to work?"

Kayla nodded as her full lips turned slightly upward.

When they went into the house, Kayla's eyes darted around the hallway, landing on framed pictures of Simon and Deena, smiling, laughing, sitting with friends. She had the look of a hungry kid staring at a pastry shop window as she peered at the dining room to the right and looked with curiosity down the hall toward the kitchen.

"Right this way," said Deena, leading the way into the living room.

Kayla sat down on the couch and crossed her legs. Uncrossed them. Placed her hands on her knees. Took them off. Crossed her arms. Sat on her hands. Crossed her arms again. It was quite the display.

"So tell me," said Deena. "What have you learned about Ophelia after having read the play?"

Kayla quickly came alive, excited to share her opinion. And there were no more worries about a single one of her appendages. She chattered away about Ophelia and the play, but Deena barely heard a word. She was too busy watching a new Kayla come into view.

93

———

The coaching session was scheduled for an hour, but things were going so well that they went to four p.m. Kayla was unrecognizable from the shy girl who'd shuffled into the room two hours before. Her shoulders were no longer hunched; she looked directly at Deena when she spoke, and her eyes were bright and alert.

"That was awesome, Mrs. Bartlett. I can't wait for next week."

"Great," said Deena, laughing, "but I see it's getting late. You should let your mother know you're ready to be picked up."

Kayla's eyes lost a bit of their luster as she pulled out her cell. When her mother answered, her face went from anxious to upset to beaten down.

"But Mom . . . I know, but we were only . . . I didn't mean to. Honest . . . Can't you please—Hello? . . . Hello? . . . Mom?"

Kayla ended the call with her back turned. Her shoulders were pulled up around her ears and her hands were reaching for her face as she let out a sob. Deena took a tentative step in her direction and placed her hand on Kayla's shoulder. That one act of kindness was more than the girl could handle. Kayla bent over and, with her body shaking, started to cry.

"Oh my goodness, Kayla." Deena turned the girl around. "Come here."

Deena led her to the couch, and they sat together until Kayla's crying slowed. "Would you like to tell me what happened?" asked Deena. "Is there anything I can do?"

Kayla wiped her tears with the back of her hand. "My mom gets angry when I keep her waiting. I think it's because she hates that I want to be an actor. She got me a part-time job bussing tables where she works over at the Shelby Bar & Grill, and when I graduate, she wants me to work full-time, help out with the bills." Kayla looked

into Deena's eyes. "But I can't do that, Mrs. Bartlett. I hate it there."
The tears started up again. "She—she said if I want to waste my time
acting, I can find my own ride home."

Poor kid, thought Deena. She didn't have the kind of support
Deena had been lucky enough to have, and still she stayed focused
on what she wanted. Kayla was stronger than Deena had imagined.

"How about if I have a conversation with your mother? Tell her
how talented you are. I'm sure once she understands what you're
trying to do, she'll support you."

Kayla flinched as she twisted the hem of her shirt. "Oh, no. Please
don't. She gets really mad sometimes. Promise you won't say anything."

Deena examined the panic in Kayla's face. There had to be something she could do, but for now it was probably best to bring the
temperature down in the room.

"All right, we can figure something out later. Stay for dinner and
I'll drive you back after."

"That would be nice."

"Just be sure to text your mother that you'll be home late."

———

Kayla helped set the table, and when Simon got home, they all
sat down to dinner. But Kayla seemed more interested in moving the
food around her plate than eating.

"I was wondering," she said. "How old were you when you
started acting?"

"About your age. I decided to be an actor after my first trip to
New York. I was fifteen at the time. When I told my parents, they
were shocked. They couldn't imagine their shy little Deena onstage."

"You were *shy*? Really?"

"Oh, yes." Deena arched an eyebrow at Kayla and added, "I'd say, every bit as shy as you."

Kayla blushed and looked down at her plate. "Was it okay with your mom and dad?"

"My mother had a hard time with it. When I look back, I suspect she was afraid I might change into someone she wouldn't recognize. But my father was great."

"What about you, Kayla?" asked Simon. "Why acting?"

"It was, like, something I always wanted. I used to make up plays and act them out in my room."

"How great is that. Comedy? Tragedy?"

"Umm, I don't know." Kayla moved the food around her plate, took a drink of soda, cleared her throat. "Just regular plays, I guess." She looked back at Simon's kind face, straightened up a little, and said, "It's hard to talk about stuff. What I like about acting is that somebody has picked out all the words I don't know how to say. I just climb up on top of those words, strap my feelings on my back, and ride them out into the world where they can finally feel the warmth of day."

Deena stared at Kayla. *My goodness*, she thought. *My, my goodness.*

———

After dinner Deena drove Kayla to one of the few apartment buildings in Stanhope, a run-down low-rise on the outskirts of town. She hated for her to leave the car. There was no telling what would be waiting inside.

"Are you going to be all right?" asked Deena.

Kayla stared down at her lap. "I'll be okay. Mom's at work now."

"Look, if you ever need anything, just call. I'll be happy to help. It can be as small as a ride or as big as a shoulder to cry on. Okay?"

Kayla turned her face to Deena and flung her arms around Deena's neck.

"Thank you," she whispered.

The show of affection so unseated Deena that she didn't know what to do with her hands. Her body tensed as she patted Kayla's back.

Then, just as abruptly, Kayla turned, opened the door, and left. Deena couldn't help but notice that the apartment building's puce-colored paint was peeling; there were weeds growing through the cracks in the walkway; several windows on the upper floors were broken. If this was all Marlene Madden could afford, Deena could almost understand her wanting financial help from Kayla. But c'mon, a mother should want the best for her child. Deena found herself wondering just what kind of person Kayla's mother was.

As the building's door closed behind Kayla, Deena left for the trip home. By the time she arrived she'd made a decision: It would make for a very pleasant evening if she and Simon grabbed a beer at the Shelby Bar & Grill some time real soon.

16

Two nights later, Deena was trying to talk Simon into going for a Saturday-night beer at Shelby's, but he wasn't going for it.

"I think it's a bad idea, Deena."

"I'm not planning to do anything," she said. "I just want to sit at the bar and see what kind of person Kayla's mother is."

"Right. Like you can tell who a person is by watching them pitch beers."

"I'm an actor," she joked. "It's my business to know people."

Simon put down his coffee, pursed his lips, and finally said, "Fine. We'll go for one beer, but that's it."

"One beer," she repeated with a grin. "That's it."

At ten o'clock they scrambled into the car. Things didn't really get started at Shelby's till then, and Simon thought it was best to blend into the crowd. When they'd moved to Stanhope, Shelby's was one of the first places they'd checked out. Deena and Simon had a love of bars with an iffy edge—a reminder of that grungy little bar on St. Mark's Place in the city where they'd met.

It was nearly 10:30 by the time they arrived. The parking lot was packed, but Simon managed to find a spot at the far end of the gravel lot. They opened the grimy door to the bar and stepped into a throwback from their early days in Stanhope. Deena and Simon had spent a fair amount of time at Shelby's. What they'd loved about the place was the same thing they loved about any dive bar. No bells and whistles, no pretty little banter, no effort at being hip or new or cutting-edge. All that was promised was a place to order a drink, with or without your buddies, knowing that the beefy bartender didn't give a shit whether he saw you again or not. You've gotta love the attitude.

The bartender back in those days was a bear of a man named George, with thick fingers, a scruffy beard, and a voice that rumbled like an engine without a muffler. It was too bad he wasn't there; they'd really liked the guy's take-it-or-leave-it vibe. Deena wondered if he'd moved on.

There was an OPEN sign flickering above the bar. The jukebox in the corner was broken. The bar stools were mismatched. In short, it was exactly as it had been ten years ago. Of the two bartenders on duty, only one had all his teeth. This was not the place to order a mojito.

Deena and Simon chose seats at the bar next to the spot where the waitresses grabbed their orders. The stools barely managed to stay in one piece, and Deena's was worse than Simon's. When the bartender came over (thank God, the one with teeth) Simon ordered a Bud, Deena a Coors. It's smart to avoid drinks served in a glass at a place like Shelby's if staying healthy is on your agenda. While they waited for their beers, Simon elbowed Deena and cocked his head toward a waitress picking up an order from the bartender.

"For Chrissake," said the waitress in a cigarette-cured rasp, "how long am I supposed to wait for that goddamn Jameson?"

"Keep your shirt on, Marlene." He slammed a shot of Jameson on the counter and with a leer said, "On second thought, I wouldn't mind a peek."

"Fuck you."

That was her. Had to be. It was like looking through a time machine. This is what Kayla would look like in another twenty hard-lived years. Marlene was a small, wiry woman with platinum blonde dyed hair—no makeup, under-eye circles, sunken cheeks, and a heavy-smoker's pallor. But it was her eyes that showed the weight of what Marlene was carrying. They were hard and angry. This was a woman who'd been knocked around one too many times.

Deena nursed her beer with one ear trained on Marlene, who clearly didn't believe in service with a smile. It looked as if the table in the corner knew her, because they were giving her a hard time, trying to get a rise out of her.

"How 'bout it, Marlene? I'll pick you up at closing."

Without looking at the offender, Marlene threw out a quick "I'd rather eat glass," which prodded a fair share of ribbing from the other five guys. She went back to the table a few more times until a collective bellow rose up from their ranks—part anger, part laughter. It blew over everyone else in the bar, putting a stop to all conversation as heads turned toward the table, rubbernecking an accident in progress.

Marlene had dumped a beer on Mr. Smooth's lap.

"What the fuck!" he yelled, jumping up.

"Yeah," she said, "what the fuck. The next time you put your hand on your dick at my station, I'll cut the goddamn thing off."

Jesus. Shelby's was even worse than when she and Simon used to come. This was where Marlene wanted her daughter to work?

Deena had seen enough. She leaned over to Simon. "Let's go."

He nodded, paid for their beers, and they headed toward the door. But before they could leave, Deena felt a hand on her shoulder. When she turned around, she was face-to-face with Marlene. A cloud of cigarette smoke was attached to her skin, hair, and clothes, and her fingers were tinged a nicotine yellow.

"I know you," she said in her distinctive baritone. "You're that acting teacher."

Deena wanted to run out the door.

"Yes. My name is Deena." She held out her hand. "And you are...?"

Marlene gave her a knowing smile. "You know exactly who I am. What's the deal? Checking me out?"

"We just stopped in for a beer," said Simon. "Georgie's not in tonight?"

"He was arrested last May. Don't know when he's comin' back."

Simon nodded and said, "Tell him Deena and Simon said hey."

"Will do." Marlene's version of a smile disappeared. "You can do *me* a favor too. Stop filling my kid's head with acting horseshit."

Deena considered her words carefully. The last thing she wanted was to put Kayla in a bad spot. "Mrs. Madden, you should know that Kayla is very talented."

Marlene took a step closer, bringing her cloud of cigarette smoke with her. "Talented doesn't pay for shit." After staring at Deena another second, she took a step back. "When Georgie gets outta jail, I'll tell him you were here."

17

Deena decided there should be a law requiring people to sit in a chair for a week before doing something they absolutely, positively thought was a good idea. Simon had been right: They shouldn't have gone to Shelby's. Sure, he'd been quick on his feet when he mentioned George to Kayla's mother, but all he really accomplished was a little face-saving. A woman as street-smart as Marlene Madden wasn't going to fall for that kind of three-card monte.

Any minute a call was bound to come in from Kayla about her mother. And yet, not only was Kayla maintaining radio silence, but when her Thursday coaching rolled around five days later, she seemed fine—actually, more than fine—and it was a relief.

After the coaching session was finished and Kayla was out the door, Deena marched herself into the bathroom, stared in the mirror, and swore she would never meddle in another person's business again.

Deena and Simon's Shelby misadventure had at least taken some pressure off the Agatha waiting game, which put their marriage on firmer footing—just in time for Simon's teachers' conference in

Albany. Deena wasn't looking forward to sleeping in an empty house, but she reminded herself that Simon would be back on Tuesday. Four days was nothing.

To keep herself busy, she put together a long list of projects. Luckily, she could keep her visits to Wilshire at a minimum, thanks to Maggie, who had miraculously become friends with her aunt. When Deena asked her what in the world they talked about, Maggie said, "Your aunt has such wonderful stories. She just needs someone to listen," which floored her. For years Deena had knelt at Agatha's feet like an acolyte, hanging on every word the woman said. A lot of good it'd done her.

On Friday morning Deena got up at five to make breakfast for Simon before he left. With the last strip of bacon eaten, he grabbed his bag, gave Deena a kiss, and left her standing on the front porch waving good-bye like a nice little suburban housewife.

After he'd driven off, Deena went back into the house full of energy and ready for business. She had plans to clean out their bedroom closet, reorganize the desk, make a few batches of soup for the freezer, and anything else she could get her mind around. But when she walked into the foyer something hit her.

What the hell was that smell? She couldn't tell if it was a dead mouse or something else. Rotting food. That's what it was. *My God,* thought Deena. *It's awful.*

She grabbed the trash in the kitchen and took it out to the bin. Then she went back in, opened all the windows, and turned on the attic fan. But the smell remained, and it was everywhere. Best to sit outside and catch some sun until the place aired out.

An hour later she went back in, but the damn smell was still there. Actually, it was worse. It couldn't be coming from the refrigerator, could it? Maybe she should check.

Fifteen minutes later, Deena had emptied everything out and was on her hands and knees scrubbing the inside with a mixture of ammonia and water. When she was finished, she stood and stretched the kink from her back. One by one she put everything back, throwing out the not-so-fresh vegetables, just to be sure.

With all that done, she plopped into a chair before making herself another cup of coffee.

Damn it. The smell was still there, and, even worse, it was making her nauseous. It clearly needed time to dissipate. She grabbed her keys and headed to the market, figuring that by the time she got back it would be gone.

Deena pulled into her driveway a couple hours later with takeout from Mumbai Kitchen. She walked into the house and—Jesus. It was more than unbearable, it was toxic. She grabbed a dish towel and clamped it onto her nose and mouth.

This was ridiculous. Somewhere in her damn house, something was rotting, and if it took the rest of the day and into the night, she was going to find it. She got down on her hands and knees to peer under the stove. She checked the potato bin, emptied the contents of the drawers, and scrubbed inside. She even checked the inside of the coffeemaker.

Three o'clock turned to four and then five and then six. She emptied the cabinet under the sink and scrubbed the inside of the dishwasher. Then, shit. She felt her muscles seize—like the warning she used to get before a panic attack.

Why?

Deena did her best to shove the feeling aside.

Her breathing accelerated as she doubled her efforts, with her hand tightly holding the cleaning rag and her jaw clamped shut. And yet, her determined focus didn't stop the twitching of her left eye.

Just ignore it, goddammit.

Deena cleared the counter of the toaster, the olive oil, the salt and pepper shakers, the garlic container, and then wiped everything down. She sprayed the oven with cleaner, dismantled all the burners, scrubbed inside the trash bin drawer, scoured the microwave, took apart the toaster.

And yet the putrid smell grew. Her eyes were watering and she was close to throwing up.

By nine p.m. she was standing in the middle of her kitchen, exhausted. All around her—on the table, the counter, the chairs, the floor, everywhere—were the contents of each cabinet and cupboard, but still the stench remained.

She couldn't stand it.

Deena booked a room at the Marriott and then left a phone message for an industrial cleaning service, hoping against hope they could come the next day.

—

Deena got lucky. The next morning she heard from the cleaning company: They had a cancellation, and could meet her at the house in the afternoon. She waited for them on the front porch, and they all went in together.

It was like wading into a vat of chemical waste. The stench grabbed hold of her throat and brought up a rolling wave of nausea. As they stood in the foyer one of the cleaning crew said, "Looks like that smell of yours is gone. We can do a once-over if you'd like."

"What are you talking about? My God, it's vile in here."

The cleaner exchanged a look with his partner. "Don't worry, Mrs. Bartlett, we'll get to the bottom of it."

Deena mumbled a thank you and quickly looked away. *They think I'm crazy.* But this wasn't some hallucination, for Chrissake. It was a smell.

They stayed for four hours, scrubbing every surface of her kitchen. When they were finished Deena stood in the middle of the room and, thank God, the air was clean. She ignored their suspicious looks and quickly paid them. Who cared what they thought? All that mattered was that she could now stand in her house and breathe.

A deep exhaustion came over her and she decided to turn in early.

———

At three in the morning Deena bolted awake, desperately trying to find a particle of air in the room. She could actually feel the stink of rotted food in her nose and crammed down her throat. She tumbled from bed, barely making it to the bathroom in time. She flung the toilet seat out of the way, knelt in front of the bowl, and heaved.

When she was done her neck and chest and back ached from the strain. She was so weak that she couldn't get herself up off the bathroom floor.

Deena lay there, afraid to breathe, for fear the smell would grab hold of her again. She closed her eyes, willing it away, and against all odds, she fell asleep.

18

Deena woke the next morning in a fetal position on the bathroom floor, covered with a bath towel. The sour taste of vomit was still in her mouth, but at least the smell was gone.

If it had ever been there.

She wanted to get up off the floor, but every effort, every move, was blocked by heavy, thickened air. She strained to stand, strained to shower, strained to dress.

It wasn't just her body weighing her down; it was her thoughts. In the light of day she couldn't help but wonder if she had imagined it all. Whatever had happened in the kitchen wasn't normal. Sleeping on the bathroom floor covered in a towel wasn't normal. None of it was normal.

The callus she had carefully created had been ripped away, exposing the terrifying memories of what she had been going through—along with an unavoidable question: Was her DIY therapy working, or had she crossed over into the land of no return?

There was no way Deena could stay in the house. She needed just one normal day. Maybe if she was around people, she could shake the sense of foreboding that was weighing her down.

It took so long to get dressed that by the time she got to Wilshire it was nearly two p.m. Deena walked into Agatha's room and found Maggie and her aunt sitting together—Maggie in a chair, her aunt in bed, with a bouquet of yellow roses on the bedside table.

"Deena," said Maggie cheerfully, "look what came."

"They're from Lucine," said Agatha. "For years I barely speak to the woman, and now she's sending flowers. I suppose dying has its benefits." Agatha lowered her head, stared at Deena, and smiled. The very smile, in fact, that Deena had imagined on her aunt's face a couple of weeks ago. "Don't you think the fragrance is divine?" she said, slowly and clearly. "Breathe it in, dear. It will transform you."

My God. She knows what happened yesterday. Deena quickly grabbed a chair and sat down.

"Are you all right, Deena?" asked Maggie.

"Fine. I . . . I guess I forgot to eat."

"Silly girl. Go down to the cafeteria. We'll be fine."

Deena practically ran from the room, relieved to get away from that horrible stare of her aunt's. All of her questions came rushing back. Reality or hallucination. Which was which? Agatha's comment had been delivered with intent. Deena knew that at least that much was real.

When she arrived at the cafeteria she saw the old cleaning lady, Jadwiga, bent over a Tupperware container. There was a man sitting next her in his thirties, maybe forties. Hard to tell. Deena suddenly remembered the warning Jadwiga had given. *She is coming for you.* Maybe there *was* something going on. If there was any chance she wasn't losing her mind, Deena had to grab it.

She walked past the line of people standing with plastic trays, grabbing prepackaged sandwiches, muffins, and drinks. Along the opposite wall was a steam table throwing off the smells of canned gravy and overcooked chicken patties. After what Deena had gone through last night, the smells were more of an assault than anything else.

When she got to Jadwiga's table, the old woman smiled at her as if they were old friends. "Yes," she said, "I know. You have questions."

"*Babci,* no!" said the man sitting next to her. He looked at Deena with his jaw jutting out, his face haggard and unshaven.

"Now, Oskar," said Jadwiga, never taking her eyes from Deena, "why don't you get your old grandmother some tea?"

Oskar shot up, nearly tipping his chair over as it scraped loudly on the floor. He glared at Deena and growled, "I'll come back later." He walked away with a pronounced limp and a cargo of worry weighing on his rounded shoulders.

"May I join you?" asked Deena.

The old woman nodded happily. "*Zgoda. Zgoda.* And you may call me Jadwiga. Your name is Deena, no?"

How does she know my name? The woman must have overheard someone saying it.

As Deena pulled in her chair, Jadwiga said, "Ah, little Deena. So happy you've come to see me. If you had waited much longer it would have been too late. Here, my darling. Have a *golabki.* I made them myself." She held out the Tupperware container.

Deena's upper lip lifted slightly as her nausea ratcheted up.

"No? Ah, well. I understand, *koteczek*—my little kitten. You are tired and have too many questions. Heh, heh, always questions. Everyone has questions." Jadwiga went back to her lunch. "Questions, obsessions, transgressions, confessions." She took another bite.

"You've been watching my aunt," said Deena, "and me. Is there something I should know?"

"We all have things we must know, *koteczek.* Is your mind open to the lesson?" Jadwiga looked up from her stuffed cabbage, her head tilted, her eyes crinkled with warmth. "Because I see a deep connection between you and your aunt. It is written." She raised her forefinger with its old-woman's tremor. "This Agatha is very strong. Very selfish. Your road will be difficult."

This is a waste of time. "That sounds interesting," said Deena, "but maybe I should come back later." She stood to leave, but Jadwiga's hand darted out and grabbed Deena by the wrist.

"Did it start with sounds or tastes?"

Deena lowered herself back into her chair, unable to take her eyes off the old woman's face. "Sounds."

Jadwiga lost her smile for a brief moment as she whispered, "*Auditu.*"

"Excuse me?"

The change in Jadwiga was immediate and striking. It was her eyes, now awash with wisdom that only comes from decades of hard battles fought. "Let me tell you a story."

She put down her fork and wiped her mouth with a napkin. She then looked at Deena with a smile and said, "I am from Salitska, a small village outside Krakow. A simple, quiet place to live. Soon after my thirteenth birthday, war came. So much death. So much misery. When it ended, the village was filled with hope. Six years later I married my wonderful Alfred and we had a son.

"But the Communist government that had taken hold was not much better than the Wehrmacht. By 1953 we had had enough and escaped to America. With that leaving, we exposed ourselves to the *Sensu*."

"The *Sensu*?" said Deena. "What's that?"

"I will not call it evil, for that is an old-fashioned word. It is a hunger feeding off man's basest instincts. Greed. Anger. Jealousy. It promises life for a price—the death of someone close."

Maybe I should leave, thought Deena. But as crazy as Jadwiga sounded, she couldn't. She had to hear the woman out.

"Salitska had kept us safe from the *Sensu* because our village was under the protection of St. Gereon's Chapel, built over one of the most powerful spiritual sources in the world. The *Sensu* watches jealously over all who live within its boundaries.

"But my husband and I did not appreciate the Chapel's power. We came to the New World looking for a fresh start. How foolish are the young! A short time after we arrived, the *Sensu* gathered the angriest of its disciples and pushed them into our lives. A selfish man here. A greedy child there. Because we were from Salitska, these souls looked at us as the sweetest meat."

"Why didn't you just go back to Poland?"

"It was under Communist rule. If we had gone back it would have put our family in danger. Year after year we fought. Then, one horrible winter, after forty years of battle, the *Sensu* won, taking my family from me. All except my grandson, Oskar."

"That's a terrible story. I'm sorry to hear it, but what does it have to do with my aunt?"

"Yes, yes," said Jadwiga, nodding. "Your aunt." She leaned in closer and lowered her voice. "I do not see evil in her. She is selfish, yes, and angry, but these emotions are not enough to bring the *Sensu*. She must have done something truly sinful to bring attention to herself."

Deena thought back over the years. Agatha had been downright nasty to everyone, but as far as she knew, her aunt had never crossed the line.

Jadwiga closed her Tupperware container and pushed it aside. "Whatever your aunt did sent a message to the *Sensu*, who then made sure she would feel disappointment and pain for the rest of her life. It wanted her bitterness to grow so great that, when the time came, she would do anything to be free of it."

Deena remembered the constant rejections Agatha had suffered from a parade of men who had used her and thrown her away. Could that have been caused by this . . . thing?

"How exactly would this *Sensu* free my aunt from pain?"

"By promising a healthy life in exchange for one final evil act. It wants your aunt to destroy someone. Someone close. You."

No. This is too far-fetched.

"You feel it, don't you?" said Jadwiga. "Weakness. Fear. She is taking your strength. You, the person with whom she has the strongest bond. She is doing it by attacking each of your senses, one by one. When she is finished—when all five senses have been attacked—your aunt will be strong, and you, my little *koteczek*, will be an empty shell, ready for whatever use the *Sensu* has for you. When it is through, you will die."

"This is very interesting, Jadwiga," said Deena. "But honestly, I have to go."

"I understand, *koteczek*. The world laughs at ancient beliefs. But before you go, let me ask—has anything else happened that you cannot explain?"

Deena looked away.

"I see it has," said Jadwiga. "Something you tasted? Something you saw?"

"It was a smell. A horrible smell."

"Ah," said Jadwiga. "First *Auditu*. Then *Odoratu*."

"I don't understand what you're saying."

"Each of your aunt's attacks is led by a different soldier. Their ancient names are *Visu*, *Auditu*, *Tactu*, *Gustu*, and *Odoratu*. Sight, Hearing, Touch, Taste, and Smell. When did *Odoratu*'s attack happen?"

"Two days ago."

"Good, good. It is too late to see the mark of *Auditu*, but *Odoratu*'s mark will still be there."

"What mark?"

"Each time one of your senses is attacked, your body is branded with a mark that remains visible for no more than five days. *Odoratu*'s attack is just two days old. You will still be able to see its mark. But do not fear, there is still time to save yourself. You have not yet been visited by *Tactu*—Touch, the most powerful of all. When *Tactu* attacks, it brings the other four senses with it. You would then be branded by all five marks. Once that happens, it is . . . difficult to set yourself free."

Jadwiga untied her scarf. There, around her neck, were five angry scars, and for a moment Deena saw a young Jadwiga wielding a knife, digging deeply into her flesh, her face in a silent scream, blood staining her hands, dripping down her neck—her carved skin, like hunks of raw meat, falling away.

As quickly as the vision appeared it was gone, leaving behind five deep folds and wrinkles circling Jadwiga's neck.

"I lost everything. Don't let it happen to you."

Deena recoiled and then reflexively stood.

"I—I've got to go," she said again.

Deena couldn't get home fast enough, desperate to see if a mark had been left on her body. The thought made her want to peel off her skin.

She walked through the door, ran to the bedroom, and stripped naked. She examined her legs, her neck, her stomach, her breasts. All clear. She moved to her shoulders. Still fine.

Then she checked her inner thigh. There, in an almost baroque calligraphy, tattooed deeply in black and red, was the letter O.

Odoratu.

INTERLUDE
IN FIVE ACTS

ACT I

1953

Agatha was hopping mad. She'd been waiting at the Bustleton Avenue Public Library for nearly an hour—not an easy feat for a nineteen-year-old—but Nabil hadn't shown up. When she got back home, she stomped into the house and ran upstairs to her sister's room.

"Where were you, Zahra? I waited for you and Nabil forever."

Zahra sat at her desk fumbling with a pencil. "Nabil never came," she said, keeping her eyes focused on her hands.

Nabil Abdel's no-show was the latest in a string of late arrivals and flimsy excuses. This was the last straw. After sneaking out for a year and a half, you'd think he would treat Aggie with a little more respect. It also made her blood boil the way he wasted Zahra's time. Aggie's sister had better things to do than pretend to date Nabil, just to bring him to their secret meeting places. At twenty-four Zahra had her own life to live.

They wouldn't be in this mess if her parents had allowed Agatha to date Nabil in the first place. So what if he was ten years older? They were in love.

Aggie threw herself onto Zahra's bed, ready to let loose with a tirade on how stupid their parents were, when she noticed the worry on Zahra's face.

"Hey, are you okay?" she asked.

Zahra put down her pencil and looked at Aggie.

"I don't want to do this anymore," she said. "I hate lying to Mom and Dad. They're gonna find out."

Aggie suddenly felt guilty. She was so focused on dating Nabil, she'd never thought for a second about the spot she was putting her sister in. *How could I do that?* She loved Zahra more than anything. Everybody did. Her sister was kind and sensitive, not to mention beautiful—tall and dark with sultry eyes. Her looks were a stark contrast to Agatha's, who had inherited the worst from each parent—her father's round face and large nose and her mother's five-foot-two-inch frame. But Agatha's fiery disposition somehow complemented the serenity Zahra wore like a finely embroidered dress.

Aggie decided it was time to stand up for herself. She was nineteen, for goodness' sake. Once her parents saw how much she and Nabil loved each other, they wouldn't stand in their way.

"I can fix this, Zahra. Trust me."

———

She arranged to see Nabil the next day at the Mayfair Diner—one of their favorite places to meet. Whenever Zahra dropped him off, Agatha and Nabil would spend time at the movies or take walks in Pennypack Park. They'd even go to Lovers' Lane. As tender and loving as Nabil was, he never once pushed her to go *all the way*, which made Aggie love him all the more. Still, the windows on his '49 Dodge steamed up something awful.

She sat in a booth toward the back of the diner, waiting. Aggie was so proud of herself to have arranged a meeting without Zahra's help that she got there way before their agreed-upon time of eleven a.m. Every few minutes she checked the hands on the clock hanging above the counter, willing them to go faster, but when eleven o'clock finally came there was no Nabil in sight. Fifteen minutes turned into a half-hour, and then forty-five minutes, but the only thing that arrived was the anger Agatha could feel clouding over her good mood.

And then Nabil walked in.

"Where were you, Nabil? I've been here for almost an hour." Agatha realized she was grinding her teeth and quickly released the tension in her jaw. Her parents said it wasn't ladylike when she lost her temper, but how do you stop a runaway horse?

Nabil checked his watch as he lowered himself into the booth.

"Say something," she said, raising her voice.

"Aggie, please. Not so loud." Nabil glanced nervously at the table next to them.

She closed her eyes and took a breath, hoping to smooth away the edge in her voice. "I think we should tell my parents we're dating."

Nabil's eyebrows shot up. "What's the rush? Maybe . . . maybe we should see what your sister thinks." And again he checked his watch.

"Are you *late* for something?" said Agatha sarcastically.

"No, no. I just—"

"What, Nabil?" Aggie noticed him look past her toward the diner door and, twisting around, saw Zahra walking toward them. At the sight of her sister's pained expression, Agatha's anger gave way.

"What's happened, Zahra?" she said, her voice softening. "Is everything okay?"

Her sister sat next to Nabil and fidgeted with her handbag. "Aggie, we—we have something to tell you."

A sudden catch in Agatha's stomach squeezed up into her chest. "Oh, no. It's Mom and Dad, isn't it? They figured out what's going on. Geez, Zahra. How bad is it?" This was all her fault; she'd put Zahra in a terrible spot.

"No, Aggie. It's not Mom and Dad." Zahra looked at Nabil as he took her hand.

Then Nabil turned to Agatha and said, "Zahra and I are getting married."

Agatha felt a flash of heat in her cheeks as the chatter in the diner receded. She stared at Nabil—his eyes focused on her face, waiting for her reaction. She had no idea how long they sat there looking at each other until she heard herself say, "You're what?"

"Aggie, darling," said Zahra, "I'm so sorry. It just happened."

Agatha turned to her sister, confused. "I don't understand."

"Don't blame Zahra," said Nabil. "It was me. I just couldn't—"

"Wait." Agatha raised her hand and noticed it was shaking. She quickly put it back down on the table. "You're getting married. You. And Zahra." She looked back at Nabil, searching his eyes for some kind of explanation. "What about us? You *love* me."

Nabil looked away.

"We both love you," said Zahra, reaching across the table for Agatha's hand. "And you're young. Soon you'll meet someone and—"

"Stop." Agatha pulled her hand away. "Just stop talking."

They sat in terrible silence as the chatter in the diner filtered back in. Agatha looked at her sister and then at Nabil as the full understanding of what had happened became clear. Canceled dates. Late arrivals. It all made sense. Aggie suddenly felt as if her insides were going to burst through her skin. She clenched her napkin to keep from lunging at her sister. Then she lowered her head and, without taking her eyes off Zahra, hissed, "You . . . slut."

Zahra gasped.

"Aggie!" said Nabil.

She whipped her head toward Nabil with her lip curled and her nostrils flared. "And you! You're a worm. Spineless, worthless. You led me on! What happened, Nabil? Huh? Were you too weak to resist the beautiful Zahra? All the boys love Zahra. Ask her how many boys she's been with. Go ahead, ask her." And then a thought came to her. "Ohhh, now I get it. You never wanted ugly Agatha. You dated me to get close to her!"

"Please, Aggie, stop," said Zahra.

"And Zahra! My loyal sister," spat Agatha. "How could you? *How could you?* I would have gone through fire for you. I would have cut off my arm before betraying you. Look at you sitting there all sad and sorry. But it's a lie. You're nothing but a pretty face slapped onto a slithering, belly-crawling snake! I will never forgive you. You can both burn in hell!"

Aggie jumped up, grabbed her bag, and ran out the door.

ACT II

1969

Agatha sat at the bar with her boyfriend, Michael, in his restaurant on East 52nd. It was one of those dark places in Midtown where expense-account lunches racked up tabs for sixty-dollar steaks and enough martinis to help the players forget the dreams they'd sacrificed on the way to their anesthetized lives.

"C'mon, hon," he said. "Stop being so stubborn."

"For Chrissake, give it a rest. A once-a-year visit at Christmas is all my family deserves. I get to worship at the feet of my parents, pretend to stomach my sister, and wag a finger at their mousy little daughter."

Agatha had been with Michael for a year now. They had a great relationship. Who cared if he was married?

"Well, when your friend Lucine told me how close you used to be to your sister, I thought it was a damn shame. You were all of nineteen when that business happened with your old boyfriend. You can't still be upset." Michael put down his drink and took Agatha's hand. "Don't look at me that way. I didn't tell Lucine a damn thing about the heart-wrenching saga of your sister's betrayal."

"And that's the way I want it. I'm beginning to regret telling you." Agatha lit another cigarette and took a deep drag.

"Your anger has cost you friends. Doesn't that bother you?"

"They were morons."

Agatha hated thinking about it. If she could have moved to New York at nineteen she would have, but it's hard to pull off with no money and no job. For more than ten years she'd endured every damn holiday with her insufferable family until she had enough money to leave. And sure, she'd lost a few friends along the way. Who cares? Collateral damage is a bitch, but that doesn't stop it from happening.

"Even if you don't want to be around Zahra," continued Michael, "at least have a relationship with her daughter."

"Deena? Oh, please. She's nothing but a bland, nervous little blob. I can't think of anything more boring."

"Think about it, Aggie. A trial run at reconciliation without having to deal directly with your sister."

Agatha was looking at Michael's expectant face when a thought came to her. She could take Deena in hand. Not a bad idea. There were so many ways it could play out before the lovely Zahra woke up wondering what the hell had happened to her daughter.

"You may have something there, Michael. Maybe I'll invite Deena this weekend just to see how it goes."

Michael leaned in and gave Agatha a kiss. "That's my girl."

———

Agatha looked at Deena across the table at Maxwell's Plum and couldn't keep quiet another second.

"Deena, for God's sake, don't you see where you are?"

The girl was hopeless. Here they were at the hottest restaurant in town, and all she could do was stare at the tablecloth. It was excruciating.

Agatha took another sip of her scotch and assessed the fifteen-year-old. She wasn't as pretty as Zahra—her eyes weren't as beautiful, her nose a bit too large. And where the hell did she get that dress?

But Agatha had to admit how satisfying it had been at the theater last night. She couldn't wait for Nabil to find out that she'd taken his innocent daughter to see *Hair*. The look on Deena's face at the end of Act I when the cast stood naked onstage, her eyes popping, her jaw dropped—well, it was priceless. Still, Agatha had to get through the rest of the weekend without dying of boredom. The girl had no interests, no curiosity.

Jesus, thought Agatha, *look at her trying to figure out what to have for dinner.* She should have taken Deena to a hot dog stand.

When the waiter arrived Agatha made a wager with herself about what Deena would order. A hamburger, most likely. Or maybe turkey.

"May I take your order?" he asked.

Deena sat with her face lowered, staring at the menu.

What in God's name is she doing—studying for an exam?

Deena finally straightened up, took a breath, and said, "I'll have . . . the frog legs."

Well, well. What have we here?

ACT III

1977

Agatha sat on her bed with a cigarette smoldering in an ashtray by her side. The television was droning on about something, but after what had happened with Michael two days ago, she heard none of it. *That son of a bitch*, she thought. Nine years. She'd been with the man nine years, and here she was, forty-three, with nothing. How could she have believed his lies?

She started crying again, hating herself for it. *What the hell good does crying do?* Tears or not, the issue still remained.

No one ever chose *her*. Agatha was the abandoned one. Unwanted. Unloved. She had spent nine years with a man who divorced his wife and then married another woman, all behind her back. It was more than she could bear.

Worst of all was Michael's justification. He'd said that since she'd never *asked* him to get a divorce, he had assumed it didn't matter.

Agatha was nothing but a piece of trash.

Thank God, she wouldn't have to spend another night alone. Deena was waiting for her in the living room. Agatha just needed to pull herself together.

The past eight years with Deena hadn't worked out as she'd planned. In the beginning, she'd embraced her niece's education with gusto, cramming in as many sketchy experiences as possible during her weekend visits. It was New York's diverse underbelly that had done the heavy lifting. Password-protected clubs down dark alleyways. Illicit rendezvous in the bathrooms at Club 82. The backroom at Max's. While the hoped-for glimpse of Andy Warhol and his entourage hadn't materialized, the newest darling, Le Clique, had come through with their gold-painted dancers and air of debauchery. What gratified Agatha the most was that poor, dear Zahra was so burdened with guilt, she couldn't bring herself to ban Deena from coming.

Of course, not everything had panned out. Agatha's plan for Deena's multi-partner sex and drug-fueled life hadn't left the starting gate. The problem was simple. When their weekends together were over, Deena would toddle back to her parents, where their morality held sway.

It was just as well. As time passed, she and Deena developed a relationship. Her niece took up many of Agatha's interests. The theater, of course, as well as a love of food and wine and museums. Agatha had had a hand in who Deena had become, and over time she had learned to enjoy the girl's company.

At 8:30 p.m. she pushed away thoughts of Michael, forced herself out of bed, and pattered into the living room where Deena was waiting. After finishing their dinner from Wang Fu's they were blindsided by a citywide blackout. It was too much. The final straw. To Agatha's embarrassment, she felt a catch in her throat.

"Are you okay?" asked Deena.

"That, my dear Deena, is a question best saved for another day. But I will say this: The cesspool that New York has turned into matches my disaster of a life."

Agatha couldn't stop the tears. *Shit.* She hadn't cried in front of anyone since she was nineteen. If she'd been prepared, it wouldn't have happened. It was that damn comment of Michael's replaying in her head . . . *assumed it didn't matter* . . . *assumed it didn't matter.* The more she thought about it, the more the tears came. What made it worse was that she was crying in front of her niece.

She took a long drag from the last of her cigarette, feeling the nicotine bring her mind back into focus. As the smoke curled into the room she glanced at Deena and saw something she'd never bothered to notice. Beneath her niece's uncomfortable face, behind the tense shoulders and wrinkled brow, lived a deep concern for Agatha's well-being. And something more: love.

"It's Michael," said Agatha, quickly averting her eyes.

"What happened?"

"Let's just say that Michael and I have reached a parting of the ways."

"Oh my God, Aunt Agatha, I'm so sorry."

And that's what did it. Agatha cried and cried, unable to hold her emotions in check any longer. When she finally looked up, Deena was standing in front of her with a glass of water. The consolation of that small gesture surprised and unsettled her—and yet, it meant everything.

Deena sat next to her and quietly said, "Would you like to tell me what happened?"

Agatha suddenly felt uncomfortable with this reversal in their relationship. This wouldn't do. It wouldn't do, at all.

"Actually, no," she said. "But now that you mention it, I have something else I'd like to share—a piece of advice that will help you now that you've moved to New York."

Agatha lit another cigarette and took a deep drag to chase away the last of the weakness she'd allowed to enter the room. Then she leveled her eyes at Deena, gave her a half-smile, and in a quiet voice said, "Do it to them before they do it to you."

Even in the half-light Deena's concern shone through. Here was someone Agatha could spend time with, share a meal, have a conversation. She didn't need some lying bastard pretending to be a human being just to rack up a few hours in the sack. Agatha had Deena. They could go to the theater, maybe even take a vacation together. For once in her life Agatha didn't feel alone.

A relationship with her niece. Who would have thought.

ACT IV

1987

Agatha paced her living room floor, trying to walk off her anger. Deena and Simon, the newest man in her neice's life, had just left and Agatha was having a hard time keeping herself in check. Everything she'd worked toward over the past ten years was in jeopardy of being destroyed.

I will not *be abandoned again. I will not be the unwanted one, the reject.*

She saw how Deena and Simon looked at each other. This was different from the other losers Deena had dragged in. The guy actually had a job, dressed well, bathed.

This can't be happening.

Agatha had been good to Deena, patient and supportive. She'd introduced the girl to producers and directors. If it hadn't been for her, Deena wouldn't have half the career she had.

Now that Agatha was in her fifties she'd given up any hope of a permanent relationship. After her debacle with Michael she'd played the musical chairs dating game, hoping she'd be the one left with a seat. The idea of growing old alone terrified her.

That's why people have children. They're supposed to be there for their parents. Always.

But it was more complicated than that. On the one hand, she had developed a real affection for Deena. Whenever the man of the hour hurt her, it was Deena who stepped in, ready to fill the void. On the other hand, she'd hated Zahra and Nabil for so long, it had become its own kind of relationship. When they had died eight years ago, she needed a replacement. She needed Deena. At the end of the day Agatha didn't know if she loved her niece or hated her. It was probably a little of both.

The important thing was that Deena remain by her side, exclusively and always. She was finished sharing; she was done being second in line. Deena was hers, and she was going to keep her any way she could.

But if Deena left her—if she made the mistake of getting married—Agatha would do everything in her power to make her niece's life a living hell.

ACT V

2001

Agatha stood at the open door to Deena and Simon's Tribeca apartment, assessing the wreckage of boxes piled high in the middle of the room. It made her sick to her stomach.

"Agatha," said Simon, coming into the living room. "You made it."

"How else am I expected to see you off? You won't bother coming to my place."

Deena rolled her eyes as she gave Agatha a hug. "C'mon, Aunt Agatha. We're in the middle of packing. The movers will be here first thing in the morning and we're not even close to being ready."

Agatha slowly walked across the bare hardwood floor, sat in a chair by the window, and pulled out a cigarette. "Aren't you going to offer me a drink?"

"Oh. Well, sure, but all the glasses are packed. I'd have to give it to you in a paper cup."

Agatha couldn't count the number of times she'd told Deena that paper cups were for lowlifes. It was yet another slap in the face doled out to the one person who had single-handedly changed her ungrateful little life.

"Forget it," said Agatha as she lit her cigarette. Deena offered her an ashtray, but Agatha chose to ignore it, flicking her ashes on the floor instead.

"Once we're settled," said Deena, "you can come up. We plan on making the guest room something special. You'll love Upstate."

"I'm not one for the country. You know that." This was a waste of Agatha's time. She stood up and headed to the door.

"Wait. You're leaving?" said Deena. "Already?"

Agatha didn't bother turning around. "You're obviously busy. I'm heading home."

Agatha slammed the door when she got to her apartment, leaving a trail of anger in her wake.

That little ingrate. After everything I've done for her.

She'd felt Deena slipping away the very night Simon had walked through her door fourteen years ago. Agatha had lost. She would now have to face living her life alone. Oh sure, Deena talked about coming into the city from time to time. She laid it on thick, saying she'd stay with Agatha whenever she got cast in a show—just like the old days.

Well, Agatha would be damned if she'd sit by and do nothing after all the work she'd put into her niece's career, introducing her to the people who mattered.

What Agatha giveth, shall be taken away.

She grabbed the phone from the living room end table and made her first call.

"Stewart. Agatha here . . . Fine, fine. But I can't say the same for my niece. You've always been a good friend. I don't want you to get bitten in the ass . . . Sure. She did a great job, but things have changed . . . Uh-huh . . . Yup . . . Coke, pills, you name it. I know I recommended her, but that was years ago. I sure as hell wouldn't recommend her now . . . Mmm . . . Okay. Don't mention it. When it comes to business, it's best to be honest."

First call, done. Now . . . who's next?

PART TWO

19

Deena stood naked in front of her mirror, trying to grasp the image in front of her. The existence of an ornate letter O on her inner thigh seemed as likely as a scrawl of graffiti written on the wind. She hadn't wanted to believe Jadwiga, and yet there it was, burned into her flesh like a brand, coiling with all the intricacy of an illuminated initial from a medieval manuscript.

Odoratu. Smell. The second attack. The letter O was all she could see. She hadn't lost her grip. Everything that had happened to her was real.

Deena threw on her clothes, ran from the house, and climbed into the car.

She needed help. She needed Jadwiga.

Any rational person would sooner believe Deena was having hallucinations than consider the crazy story Jadwiga had told—a tale woven from superstition and fear designed to frighten children on cold winter nights, happening now . . . in the twenty-first century. The letter O in deep blacks and reds did more than make Deena a believer. It brought a rush of images to her mind's eye, detailing everything that had happened over the past few weeks. Every incident. Every moment. She had been afraid she was losing her mind—but she wasn't. And if Jadwiga was to be believed, there was plenty more waiting around the corner.

She avoided Stanhope's Main Street, with its thirty-mile-an-hour speed limit, opting instead for side roads where her reckless speed and breakneck turns wouldn't be noticed. It had only been an hour since she'd left Wilshire's cafeteria and the terrifying story Jadwiga had spun. By now the old woman must be back on the second floor, working. There was still time to catch her, to ask for help.

Deena careened into Wilshire's parking lot and haphazardly straddled two parking spots closest to the entrance. By the time she got to the second-floor nurses' station she had worked up a sheen of sweat on her upper lip.

Calm down, she thought, catching her breath. She managed to put on a smile as one of the nurses came over.

"Hi there," said Deena. "I'm here to see Jadwiga. Could you point me in the right direction?"

"Jadwiga went home early. She wasn't feeling well. Did you need something, Mrs. Bartlett?"

Keep it together.

"No," she answered. "I just had . . . a book. A book I wanted to give her . . . on Poland. If I could have her phone number, or maybe even her address, I could drop it off."

"I'm sorry, we can't give out that information. I'm sure you understand."

"Oh . . . umm, yes. Of course." Deena grabbed a piece of paper from a notepad on the counter and helped herself to a pen. "Here's my number. Could you please tell Jadwiga I was asking for her?"

"Sure."

Deena took a quick look down the hall, considering whether to return to her aunt's room.

No, she thought. *Not today.*

Instead, she went to the elevator and down to her car. Simon would be back from Albany on Tuesday. That meant she had all of two days to pull herself together.

Her drive home was a helluva lot slower than her trip to Wilshire. She lowered her speed as she drove down Main Street with its small-town comings and goings. How could the world be rolling along as if nothing had happened?

The bright sun shone through rows of pin oaks, casting dappled light on the sidewalks below. Shoppers slowly sashayed, glancing at wares displayed in windows chockablock with books and clothes and toys. There was a gathering of regulars in front of Java Joe's. Four little boys played tag on the village green as their mothers sat on benches, watching with beatific smiles at their bundles of progeny, their pride and joys, their fair-haired boys, their pets, their honeys, their angels.

And all of them, every last one of each single villager, was mocking her, showing Deena a normal life, free of fear, free of phantoms, free of battles for one's soul. She was like a bad actor in a B movie, saddled with a laughable script, destined for the corridors of cult-classic horrordom.

20

When Deena got home she went straight to her bedroom and packed a bag. There was no way she was spending two days in the house alone. For Chrissake, she'd been attacked by her own kitchen. There was no telling what was coming next.

She got to the Marriott by six and after checking into her room went down for dinner. Sure, she had a bit more wine than she should have. So what? If impending doom doesn't ring the time-to-drink bell, nothing does. After dinner she went back to her room with her edges properly smoothed.

That night Deena slept. *Really* slept. When she got up the next morning she headed to the shower feeling better than she had in weeks. Simon would be home on Tuesday. Surely she could manage to get through one more day—not that she planned on telling him anything. That would be a mistake. But having him in the house would at least provide some balance until Jadwiga helped her figure things out.

The shower's spray bit into her back, releasing the muscles in her neck and shoulders. For a full ten minutes she stood with her face tilted up, allowing the water to seep into her bones as she let out a satisfying sigh. There was nothing like a long luxurious shower to make everything right with the world.

But she had things to do. Deena needed to get to Wilshire and have that talk with Jadwiga.

She grabbed a washcloth and reached for the soap sitting on the edge of the tub—and then stopped mid-reach.

Something was happening to the soap.

Deena stood there, wet and naked, her eyes glued to an irregular quarter-inch hole forming on the soap's surface. Another hole appeared above the first and slightly to the right. Another. And another. Deena grabbed the safety handle on the wall to steady herself. One hole after another indented the soap until a pattern showed itself.

Teeth marks.

Deena took in a quick breath and lowered herself to the edge of the tub, the shower curtain straining from her weight.

Calm down. It's just a bar of soap.

She tried to force the panic away, but her hand shook as she turned off the shower and grabbed a towel.

A bar of soap can't hurt me.

She carefully stepped out onto the bath mat. So far, so good. Then she turned to the mirror . . . and let out a cry.

There, traced into the mirror's steam, was the letter G, written in a crude scrawl with trails of water dripping from its edges like drops of blood running down a wall.

Deena backed against the tile wall and slid to the floor, shaking her head faster and faster.

Gustu—Taste—was coming, and there was no place to hide.

The bar of soap fell from the edge of the tub with a quiet thud.

Deena quickly glanced in its direction, afraid to move her head. The soap was no longer whole. A large bite had been taken out of it.

Her body shook as she crouched on the floor with her arms wrapped around her legs and her head bowed down, crying in great, heaving sobs.

———

She stayed on the floor for nearly an hour. Her back ached and her head pounded. The steam in the room eventually dissipated and her body dried in the air. Deena managed to pull herself up and get dressed. She had no choice.

She left the hotel and headed to Wilshire. When she got there, she went to the nurses' station and asked for Jadwiga, but damn it—she still wasn't in. Deena couldn't bear to visit Agatha, so she turned around and headed to the parking lot.

She sat behind the wheel of her car trying to decide where to go, even though she knew it didn't matter. The incident in the hotel told her as much. Her new reality was that the *Sensu* would find her regardless of where she ended up. She started the car and drove home.

That night Deena slept on the living room couch with all the lights on. At least that's what she tried to do, but every sound and shadow kept her on point.

When Tuesday morning rolled around she dragged herself to Wilshire. Jadwiga had to be back by now.

But no, she wasn't. And the nurse on duty had no idea when she'd be coming in. What the hell was Deena going to do? *Gustu* had left its calling card with the promise that it was on its way. Without Jadwiga's help, the only option she had was to eat as little as possible.

Deena got home just as Simon was parking the car. Thank God he was back. Now all she had to do was pretend everything was fine.

———

The next two days were the slowest of Deena's life. She went to Wilshire each morning, but still no Jadwiga. And if that wasn't enough, she had to deal with Simon. She could tell he knew something was going on by the way he kept his eyes on her every damn second.

"Jesus," said Deena, sitting at the kitchen table risking a cup of coffee. Simon was standing behind her by the stove, but she could still sense his stare. "How about you give it a rest?"

"Huh?"

"Don't play dumb. You've been shooting me that look ever since you got back from Albany."

"What look are you talking about?"

"Your patented what's-wrong-with-poor-Deena look, as if I'm about to run naked through the streets. I swear to God, Simon, if you don't let me be, I really *will* lose it"

Simon slammed the cabinet door. "That's it. I've had it! And don't look at me that way. There's something wrong and I want to know what it is."

"There's nothing—"

"Don't, Deena. You're sleep-deprived, short-tempered, and as far as I can see, you haven't eaten a thing since I got back. What the hell's happening here?"

Simon stood with his legs apart and his arms crossed, waiting. But telling him an ancient entity was sucking the life out of her would buy Deena a one-way ticket to a closed ward.

She lowered her head and said, "You're right. There is something wrong, but I thought I could handle it on my own. It's—"

"Yes?"

"It's . . . my audition with Carter Wilton. I might . . ." She looked back at Simon. "I'm afraid I might blow it. My old fears could come back while I'm in the middle of the audition."

Simon examined her face. "So that's it? Nothing else?"

"Isn't that enough?"

He sat next to Deena and reached for her hand. "No one is forcing you to go."

"You don't understand. I may never get an opportunity like this again."

"Here's an idea. Carter Wilton's assistant should be back from Williamsburg by now. Call her and set up an audition."

"But—"

"Just set it up," he interrupted, with a raised hand. "If, when the time comes, you don't want to go, then don't."

Deena smiled. "I guess I could do that."

"One step at a time, hon." He reached into his pocket and handed her his phone. "And there's no time like the present."

The call was short and to the point. Wilton's assistant said she'd e-mail a copy of the play, and they agreed on a date for the audition. August twenty-third, just a month away.

The balancing act was on.

With her call ended, Simon grinned. "Now," he said, "how about a little something to eat?"

"I ate earlier," she lied. "I'm not hungry."

"Humor me. A scrambled egg is practically nothing."

Without waiting for an answer, Simon got eggs and butter from the fridge and bellied up to the stove.

Deena felt the urge to bolt. For the past two days she'd managed to get by with a nibble of this and a crumb of that, each time bracing for the worst, and yet now, in less than five minutes, Simon would present her with a plate of eggs and expect her to eat.

"Voilà," he said with a flourish, handing her a fork.

Her nerves took over as she stared at the steam rising from the plate. The deep yellow of the eggs practically pulsed with ancient menace. Nausea rose up from her stomach as she breathed in the intense smell of sulphur. Her mouth suddenly felt dry. This wasn't food; this was toxic waste. Deena did her best to control the trembling of her hand as she poked at the mound with a fork, like a kid poking a carcass with a stick.

"Simon," she said, without taking her eyes off the eggs, "I can't."

"One bite. That's all I ask."

Deena forked up a small amount and brought it to her mouth. She felt heat rising up to her cheeks and forehead, and her breathing was picking up steam. Deena locked her jaw into place. Maybe that would keep her in control.

"My God, sweetheart," he said, sitting next to her. "What's going on?"

She had no choice. She had to put the eggs in her mouth. It was either that or suffer the questions she knew Simon would ask. Deena braced herself, and with enormous effort parted her lips, closing them around the fork's metal tines. The eggs felt wet and spongy on the roof of her mouth as she slid the fork out. The first earthy notes were already hitting the back of her throat and tongue as she got ready for what she knew was coming.

But the eggs were fine.

They tasted fine.

Deena's shoulders slumped. "I'm sorry, Simon. I don't know what came over me."

"Don't worry about it. Get a little food in your stomach and then we'll talk. Here. Let me get you a piece of toast."

Deena risked another forkful, but as hungry as she was, she forced herself to take her time. Slowly, tentatively, she hazarded another taste, and another. Simon dropped a piece of toast on her plate and Deena carefully bit down.

God, it tasted good, crunchy and buttery. When her plate was finally empty, she smiled weakly at Simon and said, "I guess I was hungry."

"More?" he asked.

"No, I'm good. Thanks."

Simon stood and took her hand. "C'mere, you."

He brought her in close, held her face, and gently pressed his lips to hers.

Safe, she thought.

Deena wanted to get lost in him—be carried away to anyplace but there. She offered herself up as Simon's arms grew tighter. Her breathing came in long, deep sighs—her parted lips against his, her cheeks, warm with the want of him. Deena could taste his . . .

Taste his . . .

Her face suddenly tightened.

No, no, no.

She wrestled herself loose, but it was too late.

"Deena! What's wrong?"

The kiss! It was the kiss—bringing with it a vile coating, thick and greasy. It took over the inside of her mouth and, with each breath, bloomed with the rancid taste of decaying meat. No, it was worse than that. It was fecal—attacking the back of her throat and tongue with a bite so noxious, she imagined the inside of her mouth foaming with the poison of it.

"Water," she croaked.

Simon ran to the sink and filled a glass as Deena grabbed onto the back of a chair for support. She seized the glass and took a gulp.

But the putrid taste was in the water, liquefied and sliding down her throat. Her hand shot up to her neck as if she could claw the water out.

"What the hell is wrong?" said Simon, alarmed.

"A taste," she managed to say. "A horrible taste. I can't—"

Deena lost her grip on the chair and knocked her coffee cup over as her head landed on the table with a crack. But she didn't feel it. Every breath she took was tainted with the thick taste of decay and death.

She lifted her head, craning forward to force more air into her lungs, but her tongue was beginning to swell, threatening to block her airway.

"Hold on!" said Simon.

He picked Deena up and rushed outside to the car. She tried to stay calm but was close to passing out. When the car lurched forward, every bump and curve seemed to ratchet up her panic as she struggled to hold on.

The next thing she knew, Simon was carrying her into the emergency room of Hillcrest Hospital.

"I need help here!" he yelled.

And that's when Deena passed out.

21

Bright lights. Garbled words. Cool sheets.

"Deena, can you hear me?"

Can't speak. Can't move.

Off in the distance a woman appears. Her black hair against the palest of skin flows as sweetly as blackberry jam on freshly baked bread. The deep brown of her eyes reaches through the darkness toward Deena, lying motionless on the ground.

It's her mother, wearing a diaphanous dress the color of thinly sliced lemons held up to the sun. The fabric swirls around her as she floats closer to the spot where Deena lies. When she reaches her daughter she bends down, places her cupped hand over Deena's cheek, and brings her lips in so close, Deena can hear her breathe—like listening to the ocean inside a conch shell. She strains to understand what her mother is saying.

"Find her," whispers Zahra. "Find Jadwiga."

———

Deena woke with a start in the familiar setting of a hospital room, only this time *she* was the one in a horizontal position. Lights, harsh and bright. Muffled voices through an intercom. Beeping and footsteps and the antiseptic smells of the sick.

"There's our patient," said Simon.

"How long have I been here?"

"About an hour. You had quite the allergic reaction, but it was nothing a shot of adrenaline couldn't fix."

"Allergic reaction," she slowly repeated. "To what, exactly?"

"They think it was eggs—the last thing you ate. You've probably been allergic all your life, but your body couldn't keep up the fight. You were lucky, hon. Another few minutes and it would've been too late."

Allergic reaction, my ass. Deena knew exactly what was going on. And just like that, the fear she'd been dealing with fell into formation, ready to march her into the dirt. She saw Simon's eyes move from her face to her hand. Damn it, it was shaking again. And worse, that old acceleration-tango of her heart had kicked into gear, getting faster, warning her that a panic attack had left its hiding place and was crawling steadily toward its mark. She had to block it, beat it back into its cave.

Deena placed her hand on her stomach and took slow, deep breaths—in through the nose, out through the mouth.

"Take it easy," said Simon, placing his hand on hers. "Just keep breathing. You're gonna be fine."

But she wasn't. Not by a long shot. Deena was being hunted and there was nothing she could do about it.

When the color came back into her face, Simon brushed away a lock of her hair.

"Better?"

She nodded.

He took charge of checking her out and by noon Deena was back home, resting on the couch. And there was that crushing fatigue again, worse than ever. She could barely lift her head. Thank God Simon was letting her be. She stared out the window to their front yard, trying to remember what life had been like before Jadwiga had woven her tale of demons and death—and there were no signs that her story was vacating the premises anytime soon.

Then she remembered her dream at the hospital. The one with her mother in a flowing yellow dress, whispering for her to find Jadwiga. It was the second time Zahra had shown herself. Maybe Deena was dreaming about her mother because she needed help. Or maybe it was just her guilt getting the better of her.

She nodded in and out of sleep with visions following her every step of the way. Some she recognized, some she didn't. There was Jadwiga carving hunks of flesh from her own neck, and then Fiona turning into her mother as they stood on a New York street. But she couldn't understand what the image of the teacup was about. And again . . . who was being suffocated by a pillow?

"How are you feeling, hon?" Simon's voice roused Deena from her half-sleep.

"Exhausted."

"I made soup. Interested?"

Deena suddenly realized how hungry she was. *The Taste attack is behind me,* she thought. *It has to be okay to eat.*

"Sounds good. I'll be right in."

She got up from the couch and steadied herself. She then hobbled into the kitchen where the smell of chicken soup had taken over the room. They sat across from each other, with Simon sneaking a look at her from time to time. Deena did her best to ignore him and focus on the bowl in front of her. The soup was hot and lush and comforting. Simon had even added a little lemon and mint, just as her mother used to do when Deena was sick. After two helpings she sat back with her iced tea.

"That was great," she said.

"Glad you liked it." Simon laid down his spoon and pushed his bowl aside. "We need to talk." He reached for Deena's hand. "I want to believe you're dealing with pre-audition jitters, but I gotta tell ya, I don't. Not for a second. I mean, Jesus, you almost had a full-blown panic attack today."

"Which is exactly what used to happen before an audition."

Simon's wry smile spoke volumes. He may have bought her audition story before, but clearly not now. "Who's Jadwiga?"

"How do—"

"When you were under at the hospital, you talked in your sleep. I get more out of you unconscious than awake. So who is she?"

"Please, Simon, I'm handling it. Let it go."

"No."

"Fine." Deena pushed her chair away from the table and started to stand.

"Okay, okay. Don't tell me. But before you leave, I have something to show you."

Jesus. He's gotta stop. Deena needed to get to Wilshire for her daily Jadwiga search, because if there was one thing today's little jaunt to the hospital had told her, it was that time was running out. If giving Simon another five minutes would get him off her back, she'd give it to him.

He led her into his office where his laptop stood open. It was the classic male sanctuary, with deep red walls, floor-to-ceiling bookcases, a humidor sitting on a small side table, and a pair of weights resting on the floor. He turned his computer screen toward her and said, "Look what I found."

It was a picture of Deena clutching a fence surrounding an outdoor ice-skating rink with her head flung back, laughing. "Do you remember the day this was taken?"

"Sure," she said, smiling. "Wollman Rink."

"Yup. We'd been dating, what? Four months—five? God, you were fearless. It was your first time on skates, but you knew you could trust me, that I'd never let anything happen to you."

The picture was a universe away. She was whole then. And happy.

"You've always trusted me," said Simon, "as I've trusted you. Trust me now. Tell me what's going on."

Simon's expectant look only pushed Deena deeper into a hole where she crouched, alone, desperately shoring up her sanity. She turned her eyes back to the girl in the photo and suddenly felt an urge to press her hands against her ears—to cower at the sound of that laughter, mocking her weakness. She lowered her head and cried.

Simon put his arms around her as she sobbed into his shoulder—out of fear, yes. But also for the loss of all the promise she had squandered.

And then . . . she told him.

She told him about the attacks. About the night they'd left the theater early. About Jadwiga. About the *Sensu*. About the marks. She told him everything. And Simon listened.

When it had all been laid bare Deena grabbed a tissue from the desk, blew her nose, and waited. She avoided looking at Simon, hoping he would say something, but after a few interminable minutes she couldn't stand it.

"Do you believe me?"

He cleared his throat. "Just so I understand, you think an ancient . . . entity . . . has made a bargain with your aunt and together they're attacking you to—what? Make Agatha well? Leaving you somehow vulnerable?"

Deena shot out of her seat. "I knew you wouldn't believe me!"

"Hold on." He quickly grabbed her hand, but she batted it away. "I never said I didn't believe you."

"Then what, Simon? What exactly are you saying?"

"What I'm saying is this. Your aunt has obviously surprised the doctors with her progress. I'll give you that. And I believe you've had some scares. Voices, smells, and the allergic reaction this morning. But—"

"Allergic reaction? You weren't even listening. Where do you think *this* came from?"

Deena rolled up her sleeve to reveal an ornately drawn letter G in deep reds and blacks—the sign for *Gusto*. Taste.

Simon blanched. "My God, Deena. What have you done to yourself?"

Deena stared at him for a minute, and then . . .

"Fuck you."

She marched from the room, strode out to the car and headed to Wilshire. She barely noticed the road as the car twisted around curves and corners. Deena was too busy stirring her pot.

I never should have opened my mouth.

She punched the steering wheel. *Stupid. Stupid.* She threw back her head and let out a scream. The more she stirred the pot, the more shit came to the surface. Simon's hovering, his incessant warnings, the overheard conversation with his sister. *I'll show him fragile.* Deena would fight this thing with or without Jadwiga's help. And the place to start was Agatha.

She came to an abrupt stop in Wilshire's parking lot, slammed the car door, and hurried into the building. With a perfunctory nod at the desk, she took the stairs—no waiting for the elevator today—and strode into her aunt's room.

Maggie was there, sitting by the bed. "Hello, dear," she said, smiling. "How are you today?"

"Fine, Maggie. Would you mind giving us some time alone?"

"Of course." With the help of her walker, Maggie got up and shuffled out of the room.

"That was rude," said Agatha with a smile.

"Honestly, I don't give a shit. We have things to discuss."

"Oh?"

"I know what you're doing."

Agatha slowly nodded. "Of course you do. I'm lying in a rehab center, doing my best to get better."

"Bullshit." Deena rolled up her sleeve. "Here's what's left from your latest assault."

Agatha glanced at the letter G and said, "Pretty. Is it a temporary tattoo, or did you opt for permanent?"

"I don't have the time or the patience for this charade. I know you're behind what's been happening to me, and I'm here to tell you, it stops now."

"And how, exactly, do you plan on stopping me, Deena, my love?"

Deena stared at Agatha's calm face. "Jesus, I was hoping you'd deny it; or that you didn't know it was happening. Why, Aunt Agatha? Why do you hate me? I've never done anything to you."

Agatha's smile slowly faded and, like a dog about to attack, she bared her teeth at Deena with so much hatred, it nearly took her breath away.

"You are incapable of affecting anyone—let alone someone like me. For years I put up with the stultifying boredom of your company. You were nothing more than a gnat—an insignificant piece of shit on the bottom of my shoe." Agatha sneered. "I'll tell you exactly what my problem is. Whenever I look at your face, I see your whore of a mother smeared all over it like yesterday's puke. If I had a baseball bat I'd smash it into next week."

"My mother? Everybody loved my mother. What could she have done to you?"

Agatha reared herself up and screamed, "She existed!"

Deena jerked back. Agatha had always delivered her vitriol with the calm of a sadistic surgeon. Never once had she lost control. Until now.

The last of Agatha's scream faded as Deena regained her composure. "Know this," she said, pointing a finger in her aunt's face. "When your next attack comes, I'll be ready. You will die before you get the better of me."

"Unlikely."

"Oh, yeah? Look at you. After three attacks you're still a hopeless mess. Can't walk. Can't bathe. Can't even wipe your own ass. It's a long road to Wellsville, Aunt Agatha. You're gonna run outta gas."

Agatha chuckled. "Is that so?" She pulled off her blanket, swung her legs around, and with no effort at all, stood. "Looks like you're a little late to the party."

22

Deena thought she knew fear—the bogeyman that comes, day or night, squeezing a person's entrails into a knot of insecurity, self-doubt, and doom. She could write a book on the subject after five years' worth of panic attacks that had kept her shackled to her home.

But fear is a complicated beast. Those panic attacks were chump change compared to what she was going through now.

So imagine Deena's surprise at her steady hand as she drove back home. No trembling, no nervous tics. None of the shakes and quakes of a helpless woman cowering in bed with a blanket over her head. She'd broken through her default position of terrified victim, because she now had a clear enemy—someone to fight. And if there was one thing Deena had learned from her aunt, it was this: better to fight than to wallow in a piss-pool of self-doubt.

Once she connected with Jadwiga, there'd be no reason to go back to Wilshire. When this was over, she would finally put the sounds and smells of that place behind her.

When this is over. She knew exactly what that meant. *When Agatha is dead.* The tightness in her chest quickly eased at the thought. There it was in all its ugliness, fully formed. The resentment and hatred. This was the person Deena had become; devoid of compassion, of understanding. She wished for nothing more than to see her last surviving relative die.

And if she had to make that happen herself, she would, because *no one* would look at that effort as anything but self-defense.

Deena drove past the turnoff to her street. She wasn't ready to face Simon. Didn't want to hear the questions he'd heap onto her pile. Instead, she drove another mile to Silver Lake, just outside Stanhope. The gravel crunched under the Subaru's wheels as she slowed to a stop in the parking lot. Deena stared out at the lake for a quiet five minutes before getting out and walking down to the water's edge.

Thirty yards to her left, a boy and his father were skipping stones on the still water's surface. Across the way an elderly couple strolled, hand in hand—their postures identical, their heads tilted at the same angle. She found a bench under the shade of an elm tree, sat down, and stared out at the lake.

Deena wished she could figure out when the next attack was coming, but it wouldn't have mattered even if she could. She had no idea how to protect herself. The one thing she *had* noticed was that the time between the first three had accelerated. The Sound attack had come in the middle of June. Smell, a month later. Taste had taken a week to arrive. How many days before Sight grabbed hold?

The boy and his father eventually headed out, leaving behind a stillness that settled over Deena like a mother's breath. Somewhere a catbird let loose with its distinctive call. Soon a family of ducks paddled to the shore. It would have been nice to feed them a little bread. Deena remembered countless afternoons when she and Simon would sit on this very bench with a picnic lunch, feeding ducks and laughing. She wondered if those days would ever return.

An hour later she got into the car, bracing for the questions she knew Simon would ask. She never should have fallen for his trust-me routine, but the moment he'd wrapped his arms around her, Deena felt she'd come home. Of course, she told him everything. Big mistake.

When she coasted into their driveway there was a car parked next to Simon's, and she knew exactly who it belonged to. Fred Hamilton. *Goddammit, Simon.* She should have known he'd call her old therapist.

Deena sat in her still-running car considering whether to leave. But what good would it do? Thanks to Simon, she would have to deal with Fred sooner or later. It might as well be now.

She checked herself in the mirror, smoothed her hair down, and wiped away the dark circles of mascara under her eyes. Then, with her jaw jutting out, ready for a confrontation, she left the car and headed inside.

"Hello, Fred," she said, walking into the living room. "Life must be pretty dull if you're making house calls. I didn't know that was in a therapist's purview." She gave Simon her best fuck-you look.

Simon jumped up to give her a hug, but Deena did an evasive maneuver and took a seat across from the couch.

"Fred just wants to talk," said Simon.

"It's good to see you," said Fred. "I understand you've got some interesting things going on."

"For Chrissake," said Deena, feeling herself get visibly annoyed, "we've known each other too long for the subtle approach. Let's cut to the chase."

Fred crossed his arms and threw his left leg over his right. "Paranoia is serious business, Deena. You're a smart woman. I'm sure you know that."

"Of course I do. Don't talk to me as if I'm a child." Deena was already regretting coming in.

"I need to see you in the office so we can get to the bottom of this."

"And how do you define *get to the bottom*?"

He uncrossed his legs and leaned forward. "I want to run some tests just to make sure there's nothing physical going on. We can wait for the results before deciding what to do."

Deena figured it was best to keep her mouth shut. She nodded.

"Okay, then," said Fred. "I'll expect you in my office tomorrow morning." He stood, took a step toward Deena, and squeezed her arm. "We'll figure this out. I promise."

Simon got up to see Fred out. When he came back, Deena said, "Jesus, Simon. I can't believe you asked Fred to come to the fucking house."

"Can you blame me? I'm worried about you."

"Well, you can stop worrying. I am now in the capable hands of the men in white." She turned and headed upstairs.

As she closed the bedroom door, her phone rang. A deep male voice on the other end said, "Is this Deena Bartlett?"

"Yes. Who's this?"

"My grandmother says, come now." He gave her Jadwiga's address in a short, clipped sentence and, without waiting for a response, abruptly hung up.

23

Jadwiga's grandson, Oskar, stood in the doorway looking at Deena with his fist clutching the doorknob so tightly, she half expected it to collapse in on itself like a deflated ball. She put on her most solicitous smile and said, "Hello. I'm here to see your grandmother."

"I know," he answered, with a curl of his lip.

He turned and walked back into the house, leaving Deena to find her own way in.

Jadwiga's living room wasn't what she'd expected. There were no touches of Polish kitsch, no doilies, no painted floral furniture, no bits of decorative ceramics. The room was simple, almost monastic. There was a rough-hewn wooden bench along the wall by the door. An Arts and Crafts couch with tattered cushions faced two wooden chairs, all of which surrounded a low coffee table laid with a teapot and lone teacup and saucer on a tray. Along the opposite wall was a simple oak hutch with framed pictures of a smiling man and happy children.

Oskar stood leaning against the wall with his arms crossed, glaring at the air in front of him. Deena wasn't sure whether to sit or not.

"Thank you for calling," she said.

Without bothering to look in her direction, he said, "My grand-mother will be out when she's ready."

Deena stayed in her spot by the front door as the ticking of a wall clock reminded her that she was on borrowed time.

"You people who come," he finally said. "You won't stop until you've sucked the life out of her. It makes me sick." He abruptly turned and strode down the hall, out of sight.

Another five minutes passed until, finally, a closing door echoed from the darkened hallway, followed by the shuffling of slippered feet. Jadwiga slowly entered the room with that side-to-side gait of hers. Their eyes met and Jadwiga smiled.

"Hello, my *koteczek*. So happy to see you. Sit, sit." She motioned to the couch and took her seat on one of the facing chairs. "I am sorry it has taken so long for us to meet. I have been . . . unwell."

"I'm sorry to hear that. Are you better now?"

Jadwiga gave a shrug. "Age is a train that takes us where it pleases. For now, let us turn our sights on you." She reached for a small box on an end table next to her chair and placed it beside the tea tray. "You have had another visit. No?"

"Yes. A horrible taste."

"*Gustu*," said Jadwiga, nodding. "And the mark?"

Deena rolled up her sleeve to show the ornate G on her upper arm.

"Hear me well, *koteczek*, for time is unraveling like a ball of twine. Your aunt grows stronger by the day. Tell me, what other family do you have?"

"Just my husband, Simon."

"Are you close to anyone else?"

"I have a good friend. Fiona Murphy."

"Good." Jadwiga sat deep in thought. "Let me explain. These three attacks have weakened you. To protect itself, your soul has gone into hiding. The *Sensu* will soon find that hiding place and rip it away, leaving you vulnerable to its control."

"But you can help me, right?"

"Yes. Yes. We must strengthen your soul and then we must block the *Sensu* from entering."

"How?"

"The *Invitus Ritus*—a ceremony that invites help from another. It will allow me to sit inside you like a hollow bone through which the spirits can enter. You will then have their protection—and mine, for as long as my strength lasts. Together we will block the *Sensu*'s next attack. But be warned: When it realizes what we have done, the *Sensu* will turn its sights on another."

"What do you mean? On who?"

"On someone close. In your case, your husband or your friend. Once inside, it will use that person as a pathway to you. Our task is made simple because there are only two people to protect, which we can take care of today."

"But how can that happen without their being here?"

"There are ways, *koteczek*. Do not worry." Jadwiga reached for the teapot and poured. "Let us begin. Drink this." The earthy smell of mushrooms traveled into Deena's chest, expanding her ribs so that her lungs could take it in all the more. When she brought the cup to her lips, that same sensation spread throughout her body.

"Now close your eyes and repeat after me . . . I call upon the Spirits of Light to stand guard at the doorway of my soul."

Deena answered, "I call upon the Spirits of Light to stand guard at the doorway of my soul."

Jadwiga continued. "Allow this Protector to enter."

Deena repeated, "Allow this Protector to enter."

A sweet sound came from Jadwiga's lips as she sang slowly and quietly with a young woman's voice. But it wasn't a song. The sounds Jadwiga made moved from note to note, up and down, like a swinging watch on a chain. Deena felt herself gathered up in its silver thread and taken, swirling, out of her body. She looked down on herself, sitting with her eyes closed and her head tilted back. The edges of her body faded and then disappeared until Deena became a part of the air around her. Zahra was there, waiting, as mother and daughter combined into one. Deena was in her womb now— could feel Zahra's heart beating in tandem with hers.

Deena took in the scent of her, redolent of spring flowers. Her mother whispered, "Don't be afraid. You're ready." She released her with a gentle push toward Jadwiga, who was waiting to take Deena back into the world with the knowledge that she wasn't alone.

When she opened her eyes, she found herself lying on the couch covered in a blanket and Jadwiga sitting across from her, smiling.

"How long have I been out?" asked Deena.

"Thirty minutes. No more." Jadwiga reached for the small box beside the teapot. "You are fortunate. It is rare for someone to join me during the *Invitus Ritus*. Your mother's love is very strong."

"So she *was* there. I've been seeing her for weeks but had assumed it was just my imagination."

"Just? There is no *just*. Imagination is a connection to something greater than ourselves."

Deena was warmed by the idea that her mother had come. As for her fatigue, it was completely gone. She felt energized and ready to go. "What happens now?" she asked.

"There is much to do." Jadwiga reached into the small box on her lap and pulled out a brass disk, about an inch in diameter. The disk was attached to a short length of bracelet-sized braided leather. She handed it to Deena and said, "This is for your husband. It will keep him safe."

"He'll never wear such a thing."

Jadwiga nodded and removed the disk from its strap. "Then here. Sew the disk to the inside of his pillow. Its power will enter into him when he is most open, during sleep."

"And when he wakes up?"

Jadwiga reached into the box and brought out a small cloth bag with a drawstring.

"Sprinkle this spice in his food or drink twice a day. He will not taste it."

"What is it?"

"It is protection, *koteczek*. Together with the disk, your husband will be safe."

"And what about Fiona?"

Again Jadwiga reached into her little box, bringing out a small vial, no more than two inches high, with a cork stopper. "Here," she said. "Invite your friend to your home. When she arrives, take something of hers. It does not need to be big. A scarf, perhaps. After she leaves, pour a few drops of this oil onto the item, seal it into a bag or box, and keep it safe."

"That doesn't seem like enough. I'm doing so much more for Simon."

"Simon is your husband. It is necessary."

Deena took the disk, the bag, and the vial of oil and tucked them all into her bag. Then she looked up and said, "What does this thing want, Jadwiga?"

She shrugged. "Why does the devil gather souls? The *Sensu* feasts on anger and fear to survive, for that is where its life force comes from."

"But what can my aunt hope to gain? She's seventy-eight years old."

"Life is sweet, *koteczek*. The bargain she has made is for another ten or fifteen healthy years, but what she doesn't understand is that the *Sensu* is a trickster. It has not told your aunt what happens later. Agatha will be trapped in the vines of its power for all eternity as the *Sensu* feeds on her bones."

How horrible. Deena tried to cast the image away but it was already burrowing in. "It all sounds so hateful."

"Yes. Hateful. As the story goes, hundreds of years ago the accumulated hatred in the world hardened into a single force, growing larger by the day, until the *Sensu* was formed. If the world understood the power of hate it would do anything to avoid it, for hatred and anger are the *Sensu's* past, present, and future.

Deena nodded and stood to leave. "And you've been fighting this thing for years. It's hard to imagine how you've managed."

Jadwiga quietly smiled. "It was a bargain I made long ago. I promised the spirits that I would help whoever asks and, in return, they saved my grandson. But not before his injuries left him with a lifetime of pain."

"His hip. Yes, I've noticed."

She nodded. "And something more. Oskar only sees the darkness in life. It is a great burden for him, and as much as I have tried, there is nothing to be done."

"Does he know about your bargain?"

Jadwiga sighed and rose slowly, leaving Deena's question unanswered.

"Keep watch over your aunt," she said, turning toward her bedroom. "When you see her weaken, you will know we are winning. We will talk again soon."

24

The house felt empty when Deena got home, but a quick listen in the hall told her Simon was holed up in his office. Not surprising, after their fight.

She snuck upstairs and rummaged through her closet for the old sewing basket she'd inherited from her mother. Deena had had her share of wrestling bouts with a needle. No patience. But sewing a metal disk into a pillow should be as easy as sewing a button onto a coat. She could handle that much.

The floor of her closet was stuffed with boxes and blankets and rarely worn shoes. All her promises to reorganize were wagging their fingers in a chorus of tsk-tsks as she clawed through the piles, searching. Just when she thought the sewing basket must be somewhere else, she found it wedged between a bundle of hangers and an old clock.

This was already taking too long. She had to speed things up.

Deena stuffed everything back in the closet, took the pillow and sewing kit to the bathroom, and locked the door. She sat down on the closed toilet seat and rummaged through the sewing basket for a needle and thread. Then, she split open the end of the pillow and sewed the disk along the inside seam, making sure to surround it with the pillow's fill. But not before pricking her finger twice. This was why God created seamstresses.

She blotted the blood from her finger with some toilet paper, then finished sewing up the seam, keeping one ear open for Simon. All clear.

Five minutes later, Deena was shoving her sewing basket back in the closet and placing the pillow on Simon's side of the bed. With that done, it was time to check off the next thing on her list—a call to Fiona.

Her friend answered on the first ring.

"Hello, love," she said, "How's Ms. Lightweight doing?"

"Lightweight?"

"Can't hold your liquor. I don't know if our relationship can continue."

Deena gave a tight laugh, hoping Fiona didn't notice her nerves poking through.

"How about I make it up to you with lunch here at the house?"

"Only if you serve something extremely complicated."

"Done. Tomorrow okay?"

"It's a date."

Deena needed to get busy if Fiona wanted something special. She ran downstairs, pulled out a few tattered recipe cards, and quickly made a shopping list.

Two hours later she was back in her kitchen, surrounded by grocery bags and an overfull glass of red. She heard Simon's office door close and when she looked up, saw him standing at the kitchen door with his arms crossed over his chest and reproach darkening his eyes. Mr. Nice Guy had traveled to The Land of Pissed-Off Husbands. He must have been stewing about her reaction to Fred all afternoon. Maybe she should have knocked on his office door when she'd gotten home. *Shit.*

She poured a second glass of red and lifted it like a peace offering in Simon's direction, but he stood there, unchanging.

"Look," she said, "this has been a shit day for both of us. I know you're just trying to do the right thing. Now that Fred's in the picture, let's leave it up to him. But you and I are fine, right?"

The muscles working in Simon's jaw told Deena they weren't. Not by a long shot. He stepped into the kitchen and took the proffered wine without bothering to look at her. "I don't know. You tell me."

Damn it. She needed to calm the situation down. It was hard enough fighting this *Sensu* thing without worrying about Simon.

"I wish you would sit down and keep me company," she said. "A quiet dinner will do us good."

"You don't want to talk about this?" His eyes scanned the slump of her shoulders at the question. "Fine. We'll leave everything up to Fred. For now." He pulled up a chair and wordlessly sipped his wine.

An uncomfortable truce would have to do. Deena warmed up some leftover pasta and doled it out onto two plates. And with her back turned, she managed to sprinkle a unique blend of spices onto Simon's portion without him even noticing.

———

Deena stayed up late working on the feast she'd planned for Fiona. She was disappointed and not a little worried when Simon went up to bed; he usually loved hanging out in the kitchen when she was cooking. But at least they'd had a civil dinner.

The lunch she planned was all from her mother's recipe cards. *Yalanji* and *shish barak*, and, for dessert, homemade *knafeh*. It takes a long time to make a Syrian meal. That's why Syrian women gather around a table and, like a quilting bee, prepare the labor-intensive dishes together. They laugh and gossip and brag about their sons— always their sons.

But tonight Deena was on her own. She worked until two in the morning until, finally, the table was filled with a culinary tour of Syrian cuisine. Fiona would leave happy . . . but not before Deena had taken one of her belongings.

———

Fiona arrived the next afternoon—of course, without a scarf. While it had been a fine suggestion, Deena knew she typically didn't wear them. Fiona's outfit today was a sleeveless blouse and pair of capris. Deena would have to improvise.

"Ooh," said Fiona, pulling in her stool at the butcher-block island. "*Yalan*—wait. What are they called again?"

"*Yalanji.* They're nothing like those nasty stuffed grape leaves from the store—stubby little fingers in a can. Here, try one."

Fiona rolled her eyes as she bit into the rice-, onion-, and dill-stuffed leaves. Deena liked to add lemon zest to her *yalanji*, which surely must have had Teta turning in her grave.

"Aren't you going to offer me a cocktail?" asked Fiona.

"Nope. We're going traditional Syrian. You'll get tea and like it."

It was too beautiful to stay indoors, so Fiona helped Deena bring their main course out to the backyard. Deena had set the table under a grape arbor along the side of the house, dressed in a pretty blue tablecloth and Deena's favorite melamine dishes. Any Middle Eastern family worth its salt had a grape arbor. How else would they be able to cook with the tenderest of leaves?

They sat in the dappled light and dug in.

"This is divine," said Fiona, dragging the little dough-wrapped lamb *shish barak* through yogurt sauce. "Did you grow up eating like this?"

"Pretty much. We ate what my grandmother told us to eat."

"And your mother was all right with that?"

"I assume so. After Teta died, the only change was my mother's take on my grandmother's recipes—which Mom ended up teaching me. We had so much fun. I remember Saturday afternoons making these dumplings, with my mother laughing every time I accidentally poked my finger through the dough. She was wonderful that way. Rarely angry, always patient, never . . ."

Damn it. Deena couldn't mention her mother without tearing up. It was embarrassing—even in front of her best friend.

"Hey," said Fiona, reaching across the table. "Are you all right?"

Deena grabbed a napkin and wiped the tears from her cheek. "Oh, Fiona, I was such a little ingrate."

"Weren't we all."

Deena poked at the food on her plate. "Thanks for that, but I managed to elevate ingratitude to a high art. I wish you could have met her. My mother was so beautiful. She never felt comfortable with me living in New York, and yet she supported it, sending little care packages and things for my apartment, all of which I barely looked at. My mother wasn't exactly up-to-date. A couple of months after she died, I came across a card she'd sent. Of course, it was unopened. I'd probably assumed it was one of her silly little hello cards.

"I remember sitting on my bed after a particularly tough day, tearing into the envelope and pulling out a simple card with a heart printed on the front. Inside was a lock of braided hair with a note written in my mother's beautiful handwriting. She told me that the braided hair was hers and mine, together. She called me her light, her jewel. She said that God had taken a sliver of the moon and fashioned it into the lovely woman I had become."

Fiona let out a quiet breath. "Oh, Deena, that's so beautiful."

"It is, isn't it? Now imagine this. Imagine writing that to someone you love and then waiting for a response—a few words of love in return. My mother sent that card and week after week, month after month, she got nothing. Not a single word."

Fiona reached across the table for Deena's hand as Deena kept her eyes lowered. After a few seconds, Deena pulled away from the table and started gathering up the dishes.

"Sorry about that," she said. "How about some dessert and coffee?"

Fiona gave her a sympathetic smile. "Absolutely."

They cleared the plates together and brought out the cream-filled, honeyed *knafeh*—Deena's definition of comfort food. When their meal was over and the cleanup was done, Fiona went into the bathroom, which gave Deena the opportunity to grab her handbag and rifle through.

Lipstick. *Perfect.*

There weren't many people Deena felt close to—maybe she was more like Agatha than she'd like to believe—but Fiona was one of them. She would do anything to protect her.

25

There's nothing quiet about the quiet when you're waiting for something to happen.

Deena may have felt a measure of comfort the day she left Jadwiga's, but another week had passed and the old woman still hadn't gone back to work. Deena wouldn't know what to do if anything happened to her. She drove to Jadwiga's house every day to check on her, and every day she suffered Oskar's scowl. Sometimes Jadwiga came out of her room and they'd share a cup of tea. Sometimes she didn't.

The metal disk was safely sewn into Simon's pillow, and Fiona's lipstick was tucked in a plastic bag stashed in the back of her sweater drawer. So far, things were calm. No more visits from evil entities. No more voices in the night. No smells, no tastes, nothing.

Deena could feel Jadwiga's presence most strongly in the quiet of her bed. And every once in a while she sensed her mother wrapping that distinctive smell of gardenias and lilacs and jasmine around her shoulders, as she coaxed Deena's eyes closed with a gentle good-night kiss.

But Wilshire loomed in Deena's mind no matter how protected she felt. The last thing she wanted was to drive over, take the elevator, and walk into her aunt's room. Not after their last confrontation; not after what she'd learned. But she had no choice. She was counting on Agatha's health to act as her informant, her litmus test, as to whether the *Sensu* had been stopped. There were only two senses left: Sight and Touch. With each attack worse than the last, Deena was terrified at the prospect of two more. *Tactu*, of course, was the most frightening. A lot of damage could be done with touch, and it would have the added help from the other four senses. Deena couldn't imagine what that would be like.

Going to Wilshire was clearly necessary, but Deena would be damned if she'd visit several times a week and sit in that room watching her aunt's smug face. Once a week was plenty—just to poke her head in. And if Maggie was in her own room, she would stop by for a visit. Deena's load was always lightened after spending time with Maggie, and she could use all the lightening she could get.

Over the next three weeks, Deena's schedule fell into place. On Mondays she went to Wilshire and stood at the entrance to Agatha's room. When she was awake, her aunt would look at Deena with a self-satisfied smile and throw out a small laugh. When she was asleep, Deena would stare at her face, hoping Agatha's slowly graying pallor wasn't just her imagination. On Thursdays she met with Kayla, who was starting to make impressive progress. The girl was clearly born for the stage, slipping into characters as easily as putting on a pair of shoes. In between, Deena worked on her audition for the Carter Wilton staged reading.

And through it all she waited.

As the days passed, Deena became more herself. She breathed easier, looked forward to going back to work at the Brixton Playhouse, focused on Kayla's progress and her own desire to get back to acting. In short, she was living her life. The battle felt close to ending.

The play was a godsend. She'd gotten a chance to read through the whole thing and was convinced that the part was made for her. It was set in the United States in 1980, after the hostage crisis in Tehran, a time when the country was gripped by a fear of Muslims living in their midst. The play centered around one Muslim family in Ohio and the prejudice they suffered while attending a local mosque, falsely accused of training extremists. There was a part—not a big one, but essential—of a Pakistani mother keeping her family together during the worst of it. It was perfect for her.

Deena was three weeks into her new routine when she arrived in Agatha's room to find Maggie sitting next to her aunt's bed, in tears. Agatha was not doing well. Not well at all.

Thank God.

"Oh my, Deena," said Maggie, "I'm so relieved you're here. Your aunt has been asleep all day."

Deena did her best to look concerned, but the only thing she cared about was the worry on Maggie's face. "How long have you been sitting here, Maggie?"

Maggie kept her eyes on Agatha's sleeping face and said, "What does it matter whether I sit here or sit in my room? I'm still sitting." She turned back to Deena with an uncharacteristic sadness. "As I say to my children, 'Sometimes sitting is the best move a person can make.'" She lowered her head and dabbed the end of her nose with a tissue.

"You need a break. Come with me to the lounge."

"What about Agatha?"

"She'll be fine. C'mon, a change of scenery will do you good."

The lounge was empty when they got there. Maggie settled into the couch and Deena made her a cup of tea. Then, sitting on the chair opposite, she said, "I'd love to hear about *your* family. All this time, and I know nothing."

Maggie took a sip from her tea. "Such a happy crew. You would enjoy meeting them. It's hard to imagine . . . I have five wonderful children—each more special than the last."

"Do they live close by?"

"Sadly, no. They're all in California. They had never wanted my husband and me to move to the East Coast, but Harold's company needed him in their New York office. After he passed, they thought I should move back west, but my children have their own lives to live. Besides, I'd settled in with a group of friends here."

"I can understand that. Friends make all the difference."

Maggie gave a sad smile. "Yes, we were close. The last of them died six months ago."

Deena's heart went out to Maggie. It must have been lonely with her friends gone, and Deena knew how hard it was to make new ones, no matter what your age.

Maggie raised her eyes and, noticing the sad look on Deena's face, said, "I know what you're thinking: Someone my age should live near family. When I first arrived at Wilshire, my children flew in and got me settled. Once I'm better, I suppose they'll insist on moving me to California. We'll see. We'll see."

"Don't you want to go?"

Maggie quietly stared ahead and finally said, "Honestly? My house is filled with memories of Harold. We'd made a wonderful life for ourselves here." She wiped away fresh tears and smiled back at Deena. "By the way, my children are excited to meet you. I know for a fact my oldest daughter is a little jealous over how much I talk about you and your aunt." Maggie laughed. "Trisha was always one for grabbing attention. But if it hadn't been for you, I would have felt terribly alone." Maggie took a sip of her tea. "What about you? Did you ever consider having children?"

Deena loved Maggie, but didn't feel comfortable confessing the reasons for her childless marriage. She could never have justified children after the way she'd treated her parents. Not only that—the concept of self-sacrifice didn't exactly go hand in hand with building an acting career. Deena didn't deserve children, and any child she might have had would have deserved more than she could have given.

"Simon and I were busy with our careers," said Deena. "We ran out of time."

"Maggie nodded absentmindedly and turned toward the window.

"Are you okay?" asked Deena.

"I'm very worried about your aunt. We talked about moving in together. It can be lonely sometimes, and my little house on Haggerty Hill Road has two bedrooms. There's nothing like having a friend around to open the windows and air a place out. But now . . ."

Deena moved over to the couch, sat next to Maggie, and gave her a hug.

"You needn't worry about being alone. If you end up staying in Stanhope, you can count on me. Promise."

26

Fred Hamilton was proving to be a problem. He wanted to see Deena. And he wanted to see her now.

It was a tough step to go into therapy back in 2005. Both of Deena's parents, as well as her aunt, would have put that option in the same category as skydiving. It simply wasn't done. They were first-generation Americans who had watched their parents wrestle with problems as basic as how to say "Which aisle has the bread?" Therapy was an indulgence, a mark of the spoiled and weak.

But when Deena couldn't get out of bed for days at a time, she knew she was in trouble. What had started out as an actor's garden-variety jitters turned into full-blown panic attacks over the smallest of things. It was the parade of failed auditions that had shaken her. She couldn't *buy* herself a part—not even a second look. And these were directors she'd worked with for years. With each rejection another sliver of doubt wedged itself into her sense of self until she questioned her ability to do anything.

Four years with Fred had changed all that. Deena liked his levelheaded approach. Nothing was insurmountable; everything was within her grasp. And he kept the medication to a minimum—which meant a lot. She built herself back, brick by brick, and when it was over Deena felt that nothing could shake her. The last thing she was willing to do now was return to that chair of Fred's when she knew she was perfectly fine. Unfortunately, she'd promised to play along, which meant Deena had to subject herself to a barrage of tests.

The first step had been blood work. Fred wanted to check her liver and renal function and thyroid hormone level; he wanted to do a lipid panel, HIV test (really?), and urinalysis. She also had to schedule an MRI, EKG, and chest X-ray. The good news was that it put off the brain-numbing tedium of sitting in his office, dredging up the sources of all her bad feelings and beating them like a dead horse.

The test results had delivered no surprises. There was nothing wrong with her. She could have told Fred that weeks ago, but after her conversation with his nurse the day before, it was clear that this wouldn't have stopped the other shoe from dropping. And drop it did, with a call just as she and Simon were sitting down to dinner.

"Deena, Fred Hamilton here. You've been avoiding my scheduler. We need to make a follow-up appointment."

"Let me tell you exactly what I told Suzy. I'm better. There's no need to make an appointment."

"What do you mean, 'better'?"

"Exactly that. No more voices. No more worries. Nothing."

The silence on the other end of the line was finally interrupted by Fred's audible sigh. "You should come anyway. Just to go over things."

"No."

Her one-word response must have surprised him, because there was another uncomfortable silence.

"Care to tell me why?" he asked.

"For crying out loud," she snapped, "I would think it's obvious." Deena's exasperation was pushing her voice into the danger zone. *Damn it, I need to calm down.* She released the tension in her jaw and tried again. "Tell you what. If I need anything, I'll call. Let's leave it at that. Now, if you don't mind, Simon and I are just sitting down to dinner."

And she hung up.

Simon put his fork down and combed his fingers through his hair. "You can't be serious. You're not going in? Tell me I misunderstood that conversation."

"I'll tell you anything you want if it means I can enjoy this salmon in peace."

"Jesus, Deena, why won't you help yourself?"

"How about I ask *you* a question, Simon. Why won't you let me be? I'm fine. Things are back to normal, which means there's no need for a goddamn session with goddamn Fred Hamilton, goddamn it. I've got the Carter Wilton audition tomorrow."

Simon pushed his plate away. "That's rich, using the audition to avoid taking care of yourself."

Deena slammed both hands on the table, rattling the fork on her plate and nearly tipping over her wine. "Look at my face. Listen to my words. I am *fine*. Let it go, Simon. Just let it go."

"Sure. Okay. I'll let it go." He jumped up from the table and strode from the kitchen, out the front door.

———

The next morning Deena opened her eyes to the empty space where Simon usually slept. She had assumed he'd gone for a cooldown drive the night before, but she'd fallen asleep before he got home. That is, *if* he got home.

She threw the covers off and went to the window, relieved to see his car in the driveway. He must have slept in the guest room. *Jesus,*

I don't need this right now. She had to catch a 10:16 for her audition. That gave her all of an hour to get ready.

Deena chose a simple burgundy dress with her hair swept up on top. She knew the play, had done the work, and felt she was ready. But on her drive to the Poughkeepsie train station, her thoughts were scattered. Try as she might, she couldn't stop replaying her argument with Simon from the night before. Maybe a call to her agent would help—just to get back on track.

Earl Aronson picked up on the second ring.

"Hey, Earl. Just thought I'd check in for a last-minute pep talk."

"You've come to the right place, babe," he said in his thick Brooklyn accent. "How's your head? In the game?"

"Yup. Any last words? I don't mind telling you, Wilton's reputation is on my mind."

"Funny you should mention that. I just got off the phone with Sally Pace. She worked on *Shooting Victor* two years ago. I was hoping she'd have some insight on how he works."

"And?"

"The takeaway is that you needn't worry. The temper tantrums he's known for aren't as bad as they say. What touches him off are late arrivals and missed rehearsals. Drives him crazy."

Deena laughed. "That could be said of anyone."

"True. But Wilton can be particularly vindictive . . . in creative ways. Humiliating dress-downs, spreading rumors—you get the idea. So to be clear, there can be no pleas of illness, no late arrivals, nothing."

Deena knew exactly what Earl was getting at and it was embarrassing: The missed rehearsals when her aunt had first started needing attention; those horrible panic attacks.

"What the hell, Earl. I was calling for a pep talk."

Earl laughed. "Are you kidding? You're gonna be great. Look, I suspect we'll hear back fast, so I'll follow up right after your reading.

And when—yes, I said *when*—you get the part, we'll see how the contract looks. I don't expect anything out of the ordinary."

"I appreciate it."

"And Deena," he added, "good to have you back."

She didn't know *how* she felt when she ended the call. What was supposed to be a few words of encouragement turned into a reminder of past mistakes. *Damn it, Earl.* But at least she'd stopped thinking about Simon.

By the time she boarded the train and got settled in her seat, Deena was ready to pull out her script for one last look-see. She loved the play, and while she'd never auditioned through the Hanahan, Neiler Agency, the fact that Carter Wilton used them meant they knew what they were doing.

The train finally reached Grand Central and Deena moved with the crowd up the platform to the main concourse. She walked around the famous opal-faced clock towering over the cavernous space, past various newsstands and food purveyors, and finally reached the exit.

On the other side of the heavy brass doors a sea of commuters had been released into the wilds of East 42nd Street. It was a typically hot August afternoon. Steam rose from the pavement, bringing with it the fetid air from the subway below. Gas fumes, hot dog stands, burning tire rubber, a passing cigarette or cigar—it was a stew of smells like nowhere else. The street was jammed with people pouring out from high-rises to grab a quick bite at a deli or pushcart. The falafel stand at the train station entrance already had a line of people three deep.

It felt great to be back.

She bullied her way to the curb and joined the dozens of hopefuls trying for a cab. There was no line of patiently waiting people, no orderly method of who got what. Cabs were double- and triple-parked so they could snag pushy people walking farther into 42nd Street in an effort to beat out the person behind them. Deena was no stranger to this contest of wills. Inside five minutes she was sitting in the backseat of a particularly broken-down sedan—one of the few in a fleet of yellow cabs that was slowly being taken over by the ubiquitous minivan.

She got out at 1501 Broadway, took the elevator to the twelfth floor, and signed in.

Twenty minutes later the door to the audition room opened.

"Deena? Hello. I'm Nora Henderling, casting associate. Come in."

Deena walked to the table at the end of the room and was introduced to Carol Neiler and Bill Patterson.

Carol Neiler was not what Deena had expected. She looked to be about fifty-five, petite, and very thin except for enormous breasts that were all the more noticeable with the tight V-neck T-shirt she was wearing. She had on no makeup and wore a baseball cap with the word PEACH stitched on the front and a straggly gray ponytail coming out the back.

Carol reached across the table to shake Deena's hand, her nails long and painted aqua. In an incongruous patrician English accent she said, "Hello, Deena. Good to meet you. I've read your materials. Nice résumé. I'd like to begin by hearing your thoughts on Aseel."

Deena smiled. "Aseel is no stranger to me. I'm Syrian, and while Syria and Pakistan have a complex shared history, it doesn't take away from the fact that culturally we're the same. I know where she comes from and who she is. She could easily be a member of my family."

"Good, good. Now, before we have you read, I need to tell you that we'll be moving fast. Most of the parts have already been cast. Ordinarily you would meet with the creative team, but I've worked with Carter for years and have been given a free hand in the casting of *Call to the Faithful*. Bottom line, this will be your only audition. We won't be doing callbacks."

Deena heard Carol Neiler loud and clear. The woman was doing Wilton's girlfriend a favor and had just about decided who was playing Aseel. *Damn*. Deena wanted this. A lot.

Fuck it. Whatever. If Carol Neiler had already cast Aseel, Deena might as well just go for it. She had nothing to lose.

It was like walking into a familiar room. She not only drew deeply from her past, but also from the turmoil she'd been living through since her aunt's fire—the sense of entrapment and desperation. It was all there—a boil ready to be lanced.

When it was over, Carol's reaction was unreadable. Not so Bill Patterson's and Nora Henderling's. She could tell she'd hit a home run. If Deena didn't get the part, she at least knew the audition couldn't have gone better. In fact, it was one of the best auditions she'd ever done.

———

Deena stared out the window at the Hudson River as her train headed back upstate, replaying her audition over and over again. She'd forgotten the adrenaline rush of a good performance, that sense of falling into a groove and riding it home. Surfers must experience the same sensation when they grab the perfect wave. There was nothing like it—being out of control while at the same time having complete control. Only someone striving to create would understand that dichotomy. And she wanted to go back and do it again.

But the reality of her life quickly forced its way back in as the train made its way toward Stanhope. There was too much on her plate: patching things up with Simon; avoiding Fred; and, of course, Agatha. She couldn't forget Agatha.

Two hours later she was in her car heading home when the phone rang.

Kayla's name flashed onto the display, but when Deena answered, all she heard was crying.

"Kayla, what's wrong?"

Deena could barely understand her.

"It's my mom. She—she's thrown me out. Please come. I have no place to go."

27

Deena coasted to a stop at Kayla's apartment and slammed on the brakes. Everything she'd been gnawing over—her aunt, Simon, the audition—everything was shoved aside by what she saw. Kayla was standing against the tree in front of her building, crying, and there was the beginnings of a bruise along the side of her face.

Son of bitch. She's been hit.

Kayla scrambled into the car and flung her arms around Deena's neck, crying so deeply that all Deena could do was stroke her hair and whisper, "It's okay, it's okay." While Kayla cried, Deena stewed. How dare that woman lay a hand on her seventeen-year-old daughter! She'd hoped her impression of Marlene Madden had been wrong. Just because a woman looked rough didn't mean she was a bad parent. But no matter what kind of life Kayla's mother had led, it was no excuse for hitting her kid.

Deena kept her anger to herself. The last thing Kayla needed was another ranting adult.

"Is your mother still inside?" she asked, holding Kayla close.

"She left for work and won't be back till late tonight."

That started the crying all over again. Deena waited for Kayla to calm down and then pulled her away, brushing a strand of hair from her face.

"Do you think you can tell me what happened?"

Kayla blew her nose in the tissue Deena offered, keeping her eyes focused on her lap.

"It started when Mom found my application for Juilliard. She saw it cost a hundred dollars and accused me of stealing her money to pay for it." Her eyes shot up to look at Deena. "But I didn't. I swear. I've been saving my tips from Shelby's."

"Did you tell her that?"

"Uh-huh. But it made her even angrier. She said I was ungrateful. That she'd gotten me the job to help with bills but I was wasting it on applications." Kayla started crying again. "I decided to stand up to her—tell her I was gonna be an actor. She shoved me into the wall, went into my room, and started going through my drawers, searching for money. She found my wallet and I tried to take it back, which is when she did this." Kayla's hand went up to her face. "She told me to get out. Said that if I wasn't going to help, I could find my own place to live. When I started to argue she threw a lamp at me and it smashed against the wall. That's when she said I had to be gone by the end of the day." Kayla looked up at Deena. "But I have nowhere to go."

"Yes, you do," said Deena, reaching for her hand. "You're staying with me."

It was a knee-jerk reaction, but Deena had no choice. She couldn't leave Kayla on the street, and she knew Simon would be on board.

"C'mon," said Deena. "Let's go back in and pack your things."

The first thing that hit Deena when they opened the building's front door was the smell. Why do all run-down apartment buildings smell of garbage and cat piss? But when they got into the apartment, it wasn't that bad. Their two-bedroom space was clean and uncluttered.

Secondhand furniture did its job, and the wall-to wall carpet had been vacuumed. Yeah, the cigarette smoke was pervasive, but there'd been a real effort to make the place a home.

Kayla's room was tiny and every bit as cluttered as any teenager's. There was broken glass embedded in the carpet from the lamp her mother had thrown, and Kayla's drawers had been left open after the search for money.

There wasn't a lot to pack. They stuffed as much as they could into an old suitcase and then Kayla grabbed a large garbage bag from the kitchen for the rest. When they were finished they turned to leave, but not before Kayla stopped to scan the apartment one last time. She let out a deep sigh before turning back toward the door and walking out.

The drive home was quiet—at least in the car—but not in Deena's head, where various scenarios were unreeling one by one. It would be a mistake to confront Marlene Madden, but she should at least look into whether legal action could be taken. While it was true that Kayla was a minor, she'd be eighteen in two months. Deena had no idea if that meant she was too old for child services. There was a lot to do.

Twenty minutes later Kayla was sitting in Deena's kitchen with an icepack on her face.

When Simon got home, her presence put last night's argument about Fred on hold. It was Simon's paternal smile that told Deena how much he liked Kayla, but when he heard what had caused her now-purple bruise, the smile tightened into an angry line.

Deena threw together a quick dinner. While they ate, she listened as Kayla and Simon chatted about school, and suddenly all her reasons for not having children seemed selfish and trivial. She couldn't help but imagine what it would have been like if Kayla was her daughter, and she wondered if Simon was feeling the same.

They were just finishing up when the phone rang.

"Hello, Deena, my love." It was her agent.

"Earl! You're either calling me with bad news, or it's going to be a happy night. Give it to me quick."

"If there's champagne in the house, now's the time to break it out, because baby, it looks like your dry spell is at an end."

"I got it?"

"Oh, yes."

The evening changed on a dime. Kayla managed to put the afternoon aside and did her best to join in on the excitement. Simon pulled out a bottle of Prosecco—not bad in a pinch—and the three of them toasted the good news.

At nine p.m. Deena noticed Kayla checking the time. Poor kid. It had been a tough day, and that little taste of Prosecco had probably gone to her head. Deena showed her up to the guest room and together they unpacked. Once everything was organized Deena sat on the edge of the bed and pulled Kayla close.

"You're going to be all right. Think about it. By this time next year we'll be shopping for your college dorm room, and I'll help you every step of the way." She gave Kayla a hug. "You will always have a home here."

———

Deena and Simon woke suddenly to the sound of Kayla screaming.

"What the hell?" said Simon, still half asleep.

"Must be a bad dream. I'll go."

When she walked into the room, Kayla was sitting with her back jammed against the headboard frantically batting something away from her hair and shoulders.

"Keep them away!" she shouted.

Deena turned on the light. "Kayla, wake up, sweetheart."

Kayla clutched her nightgown as she stared up at the ceiling.

184

"You're having a nightmare." Deena sat on the edge of the bed and took Kayla by the arm.

It was immediate: the connection. Like a rope attached to her chest, pulling them together. Deena followed Kayla's upward stare and then reared back. There was a two-foot-long gash in the ceiling, red and throbbing. And pouring from its opening were roaches. Hundreds of them. Large ones. Small ones. They tumbled over Kayla's head, spilling onto her lap, piling onto the floor.

This isn't real, thought Deena, but the primal part of her wanted to run from the room.

Roaches were crawling all over Kayla's face, down her neck, and into her nightgown. Deena fought the urge to slap them away.

"Look at me!" said Deena, grabbing the teenager's shoulders.

This isn't real.

The roaches fell into Deena's lap as Kayla's screams grew louder.

This isn't real.

The pile grew larger as they tumbling one over another—a sea of armored soldiers preparing the way for their leader. Because there, emerging from the center, rose a snake, coiling and weaving upwards, swaying to an imagined tune urging it to dance. It turned its head toward the bed and wove its way to Kayla's side, its scales the color of copper, its head the size of a child's fist.

Kayla wrenched herself away from Deena and stood on the bed, clawing at the wall as if she could rip herself a way out. She suddenly focused on her left arm—or rather, where her left arm *should* have been. Deena saw a snake growing out from Kayla's shoulder, writhing in the air as it made its way toward Kayla's waist. Deena knew it wasn't real but the sight of it still grabbed at her. Another snake was coiling around Kayla's leg and traveling up her body. Kayla took hold of the snake at her shoulder and pulled hard.

"Get it off!" She lunged for the water glass on her bedside table and smashed it against the side of the bed.

Deena seized her right wrist. "Stop!"

But adrenaline was on Kayla's side. She wrestled herself free and, with a large shard of glass, slashed at her left shoulder. "Off! Off!" A deep gash opened. Blood freely flowed.

"What the hell is going on in here?" Simon was standing at the door.

"Simon, thank God. Hold Kayla down while I get this broken glass out of her hand."

Kayla flailed. "Snakes! Everywhere, snakes!"

But before Simon could get his arms around her, Kayla let out one last wild-animal cry. She tore her wrists free and grabbed onto Deena's waist, pulling her in close.

The sound of Kayla's scream brought reality back into the room. The snakes were suddenly gone and a curtain of quiet quickly descended, punctuated only by the sound of Kayla's breathing. Blood stained her nightgown and sheets.

A movement suddenly grabbed Deena's attention. As she looked down at Kayla's exposed neck, an ornate letter V in lines of black and red was being drawn by an invisible hand. She grabbed Simon's arm. "Look."

Shock grew on Simon's face as he watched the lines bend and curl like smoke made solid. When he turned to Deena, his hand reflexively reached for her arm where the letter V for *Visu* was appearing with the same languorous strokes. He looked back and forth between Deena's arm and Kayla's neck.

"It's true," he whispered. "It's all true."

28

A wave of nausea traveled from Deena's stomach up through her throat as she collapsed on the bed next to Kayla. The sweat on her forehead, neck, and chest suddenly gave her a chill as it cooled in the air. She could barely lift her head.

Simon helped Deena back into their bedroom and, after bandaging Kayla's shoulder, brought her into their bedroom as well. Then he fell into the bedside chair with his shoulders stooped from the weight of what he had just seen.

"Why didn't I believe you?" he said, half to himself. "You understand, don't you? That story you told was impossible to believe."

Deena understood, all right. She'd spent weeks thinking she was losing her mind. But after what they'd just been through, she didn't know which was preferable: having a mental breakdown, or battling a nightmare that no one would believe existed.

"It's okay, Simon, I get it. But right now I need sleep. First thing tomorrow we have to get Kayla to Jadwiga's house. She'll be able to protect her."

Deena quickly described the protections Jadwiga had put into place, and as each second passed, Simon's struggle intensified as he tried to grasp this new world he'd been thrown into. When she was finished he simply nodded and wearily got up.

"I'll do whatever you need," he said, as he bent down for a kiss. "I'm so sorry." Then he quietly left and headed for the guest room.

Surrounded now by quiet, Deena closed her eyes, giving herself over to the comfort of her bed with the pillow cradling her head and the sheet wrapped around her like a cocoon. But each time she was poised to fall into a sea of dreams, she was assaulted by images of a jungle alive with menace—people screaming as poisonous plants devoured their limbs, a landscape red with blood, a corrosive river liquefying every living thing in its path. Her body cowered at each horrific image as she rolled from side to side, praying for sleep that never came.

When morning finally filtered through the curtains she dragged herself out of bed and pulled on a shirt and pair of jeans. Kayla was curled in on herself, fast asleep. Deena gently placed her hand on her shoulder, waking Kayla with a start.

"Keep them away!" she shouted. The fear in Kayla's eyes was tough for Deena to take.

She brushed her hand through Kayla's hair and said, "Take it easy. Let's get dressed and go to my friend's house. She can help."

"Hold on. I don't understand what's happening here. That was no nightmare last night. I could feel you inside my head."

Deena rubbed her temples as she tried to find the words. She didn't know how much to tell Kayla, how much she would believe.

"I know this will sound unhinged, but after what you've been through, maybe you'll believe me. There is an ancient entity trying to reach me through you. You have every right to distrust me, but I'm asking you . . . trust me now. Let's go to my friend's house. She can protect you."

"I just wanna go home."

Deena didn't expect to feel so hurt by Kayla's response, but she had to put it aside and make her understand.

"I get it, Kayla. But whether you're with your mother or with me, this entity won't stop. Please. Please. Come with me."

Maybe it was because Kayla had an actor's imagination. Maybe it was because she had experienced real terror. Maybe it was just because she was young. For whatever reason, Deena could see belief in her eyes. She nodded and said, "Okay, I'll go."

Kayla was so weak she needed help getting dressed. By the time they left for Jadwiga's, it was eleven a.m. The late-summer heat was just beginning to rise, but Kayla couldn't stop from shivering. Simon wrapped her in a blanket and helped her into the backseat of the car. Then with Simon at the wheel and Deena sitting next to him, they set off.

"Tell me about Jadwiga," he said.

Deena remembered the look on his face the day she'd confessed it all and Jadwiga had been part of the tale. Simon didn't believe her then, but Deena knew he sure as hell believed her now. It was that look on his face as he watched the letter V slowly emerge like black bile seeping out from her pores—the way he held his breath with his body pulled back and his eyes mesmerized by the magic trick playing out on her right arm.

But she was tired—so very tired. The effort to repeat what she had told Simon a month ago was more than she could face.

"Let me get some rest before we reach Jadwiga's. We can talk when my strength comes back."

From the backseat Kayla quietly said, "What will happen when we get there?"

The fear in her voice struck hard. Deena had wanted to protect her from an abusive parent, yet here she was, thrown into a situation that was far worse.

"Jadwiga helped me block this thing out. She'll be able to help you too. Hang in there."

Visu—Sight—had now struck. Only one attack was left. The one Deena had been dreading. *Tactu*.

———

It took three rings at Jadwiga's door before Oskar answered. When he saw that Deena wasn't alone, he squared himself in the doorway, blocking their entrance. "How dare you bring people here! You've done enough damage."

A weak voice from inside called, "Let them in, Ossie. There is no time to lose."

Deena pushed past him and into the house. Simon and Kayla followed, with an angry Oskar bringing up the rear.

The room was cast in gloom, with slivers of sun poking through closed blinds on every window. Jadwiga was lying on the couch with an old-fashioned icepack on her head—the kind that looked like an expandable bag with a screw top.

Deena pushed through her exhaustion, reached the couch, and sat on the edge next to Jadwiga. Simon and Kayla stayed on the bench by the door. There was an odd smell winding through the room, coming from a brass dish filled with liquid that had been lit with a wick. It was citrusy, like limes or lemons, but with an underlying scent of camphor.

Jadwiga motioned Deena to bend down closer.

"It is good you came," she said. "Now that *Visu* has attacked, the danger you have been facing is magnified a thousandfold. The *Sensu* is most vicious when poised for victory."

"You already knew?"

"Of course. I may be weak but I am still inside you."

"I was so stupid, Jadwiga. I never took into account my feelings for Kayla. Can you help us?"

Jadwiga closed her eyes and placed a hand on Deena's. "If I help your young friend, my protection of you will be far less."

"But what about the spice we gave Simon?"

"It is too late for that. Now that the *Sensu* has found its way to Kayla, she is fair game. The only way to protect her is with the *Invitus Ritus.*"

"Then let's do it."

"You don't understand, *koteczek*. My protection is not a bottom-less well. You must give up much of what I gave you if you wish to protect Kayla."

No, thought Deena. *I can't be without Jadwiga's protection with the worst coming.*

But then she looked at Kayla sitting next to Simon, burrowed under his arm. The girl couldn't take much more. She had to be protected.

"Will I at least regain some of my strength?" said Deena.

"Oh, yes. Even though we will be separated, the *Invitus Ritus* will revive you."

"Then do what you can. I've been through four attacks. I can get through the last."

Deena heard the bravado in her voice, but it didn't make her feel any braver. She felt naive and foolish. Deena thought she had taken care of everything—but she hadn't. Kayla was now at risk because of her stupidity, which made Deena feel even more powerless than she'd felt before.

Jadwiga patted her hand. "I understand what you are feeling, but now is not the time for weakness. We have much to do. Help me up."

Oskar rushed over and angrily grabbed Deena's shoulder. "That's enough! I won't have you put my grandmother in harm's way. She wanted me to let you into the house and I did, but this ritual is too draining. Take care of your own damn selves."

"Hey," said Simon, as he scrambled up. "Get off her!" Oskar squared off and faced Simon, pulling his fist back to deliver the first blow.

Deena stood up and put herself between them "Stop it! Both of you."

Oskar shoved her out of the way with so much force that she tripped over the coffee table and landed on the floor.

"You son of a bitch!" said Simon. He seized Oskar by the shirt and slammed him against the opposite wall. Oskar kicked him away and grabbed a vase sitting on an oak hutch. He lunged at Simon with the vase in his hand, poised to strike . . . until from behind, a picture frame crashed onto his head. Oskar stumbled and turned around to see Kayla standing over him with her blanket puddled at her feet and another framed picture from the hutch in her hand.

"Oskar," came a weak voice from the couch, "you must stop, my *słodki*. Please."

Oskar stumbled to the couch and knelt on the floor next to his grandmother. "Why, *Babci*? Why must you risk your life? I love you. I need you."

Jadwiga reached her gnarled hand out to Oskar and cradled his cheek. "I made an oath, and that oath must be kept . . . for you."

"What do you mean, *for me*? What have you done?"

Jadwiga gave a weak smile as Oskar pulled back in realization. "You mean, all these years . . . all those people . . . you helped them . . . to protect me?"

"I would battle the evil *Latawiec* itself for you, my little Ossie. I chose not to tell you because the burden would have been too great."

Oskar examined Jadwiga's face and in that moment he became his six-year-old self, looking up at his grandmother with tender vulnerability. Jadwiga brought him in close, whispered something in his

192

ear, and kissed his cheek. He nodded and moved to the other side of
the room, where he sat on the floor with his back against the wall.

"And now," said Jadwiga, reaching her hand out to Deena, "let
us begin."

Deena steeled herself, not knowing what to expect or how it would
affect her. "What do you need from us?"

Jadwiga told her where the tea was kept. While Deena busied
herself in the kitchen, she could hear Jadwiga in the other room giving the same careful instructions to Kayla that Deena had received.

By the time she came back into the room, Kayla looked like she
was ready to bolt. Deena put the tea tray down on the table and knelt
next to her.

"It's going to be fine," she said, her hand on Kayla's shoulder.
"You'll see."

Then she looked at Jadwiga and said, "Okay. We're ready."

Simon helped Jadwiga to one of the facing chairs as Deena joined
Kayla on the couch.

"Will I be completely alone when we're done?" asked Deena.

"Not completely, but my protection will be a fraction of what it
was. When we are finished, we will talk about other ways you can
protect yourself."

And so they began.

The pouring of tea, the incantation, the smells, the singing—it
brought Deena back to that day, weeks ago, when she'd sat in that
very room placing her safety into a stranger's hands. *A lifetime ago*,
she thought. But Jadwiga wasn't a stranger anymore. Her presence
was a part of Deena every hour of every day.

Deena gave herself over to Jadwiga's song and quickly slipped away.
She felt herself float out of her body, just as she had the first time. But
that's where the similarity ended. Jadwiga's presence split in two as
the old woman whispered, "It is time." Every part of Deena wanted
to hold on to the protection she had received against the helplessness

that the *Sensu* had ushered in. She had been crushed by a gradually closing box of fear until Jadwiga had stepped in to help.

Wait, thought Deena suddenly. *I'm not ready.*

"Yes, you are, *koteczek*. Your love for Kayla has made you ready."

A swirl of clouds blew in, obscuring her vision as Deena fell down, down, down. She passed Kayla. Simon. Agatha. Her mother. Her father. She passed everyone until she fell into a tranquil, limitless ocean cleansing her of self-doubt and fear.

Hands reached up, pushing Deena back to the surface. She rose toward the light, passing one image after another—moments of her life trapped like insects in amber. Yet still she swam until her hands broke through. One final push and Deena's head emerged like a newborn coming from its womb into the light.

She took in a loud gasp of air and opened her eyes.

It was finished.

29

Deena immediately sensed the difference—as if a set of training wheels had been taken off. She felt strong enough to push away the fear, but not enough to manage any bumps or cracks along the way. At least the weight of exhaustion had been lifted. She could feel her arms and legs coming back to life.

Deena rolled her shoulders and rubbed the back of her neck as she glanced over at Kayla, still asleep. *So beautiful*, she thought as she brushed a wisp of corn-silk hair from Kayla's face, now calm and worry-free.

And then she looked at Jadwiga. My God, she was pale.

Deena quickly stood and reached her at the same moment as Oskar. He knelt down next to his grandmother with his eyebrows forced together in worry as he gently touched her cheek.

"*Babci*," he whispered. "Are you all right?"

Jadwiga turned toward her grandson and said, "There, there, little *słodki*. I will be fine. But even if I am not, believe that *you* will. Now let me give my final instructions to Deena."

Oskar stood behind his grandmother—a sentry at his post with his hands draped over her shoulders. Jadwiga's head rested against the chair's back as she turned toward Deena, now kneeling by her side.

"The small part of me that I left behind will keep you safe for a while, but once the *Sensu* realizes you do not have my full protection, *Tactu* will attack. Of all the *Sensu's* soldiers, *Tactu* is the one that deals in reality. Its power kills because its attacks are real, and it bends that reality into shapes designed to confuse you. I must also remind you that it will gather the other four senses around it, which is what makes this final attack so deadly."

The drumbeat in Deena's temples doubled. She glanced down at her hands, now balled into tight fists, and very deliberately released them in an attempt to stay calm. Then she looked back up at Jadwiga.

"You said there was another way to protect myself. How will I fight the *Sensu* now?"

The lines around Jadwiga's eyes and lips softened. "You must focus on your loved ones. That is the most essential element needed to defeat the *Sensu*."

That's it? thought Deena as she stood up and paced the floor. Think about the people I love? She turned back to Jadwiga. "That can't be enough. I've spent years putting my aunt ahead of everything else, and it did nothing to block the *Sensu*."

"You must ask yourself if you did it selflessly."

"Of course, I—" Deena sensed Simon's eyes watching her. She looked back at him and then quickly glanced away. The answer was no. Any love Deena had had for Agatha was long gone. She had to face the fact that whatever care she'd given her aunt had come from a place of guilt. And from that guilt, resentment toward Agatha had found fertile ground. She had never once focused on her aunt. It was all about assuaging the burden of her own memories.

With that honest thought, Deena took a step backwards to the couch and lowered herself into the cushions.

"I see the answer on your face," said Jadwiga, "and your fear. Listen to me well, because it comes to this: You must find a way to believe that you have love in your heart."

Deena heard Jadwiga's words but all she felt was self-doubt.

"Embrace this truth," continued Jadwiga, "for when you do, your greatest desire will be revealed to you—the desire to protect your loved ones. That is the point. If you die, the people you love will feel anger or sorrow so great they will become vulnerable to the *Sensu*'s touch. At the very least, it will take them years to find peace. You can stop that from happening by defeating the *Sensu* now."

"I'm not strong enough to do that."

"Yes, you are," said Jadwiga. "I have spent time inside you and have seen what lives in your heart. You have carried the guilt of a young woman's actions, believing for years that you are a bad person. That is not so. Even now you are willing to sacrifice yourself for a young girl."

Deena lowered her face into her hands. She couldn't bear the thought of being looked at. Simon quickly came to the couch, sat next to her, and draped his arm around her shoulders.

"And so," continued Jadwiga, "when the battle begins, keep those you love in your mind. You are not fighting for yourself. You are fighting for Simon and Kayla and Fiona. They love you, and you love them."

"Will that be enough?" she asked, raising her head.

"You will have the same strength a mother finds when her child is in danger. The *Sensu* is unaware of this power's existence. Love is beyond its understanding."

Deena looked at Simon through her blurred vision as he mouthed "I love you." She nodded.

"And there is one more reason you must not falter," said Jadwiga. "This will be my last battle. I will not be able to help with another."

"*Babci?*" said Oskar.

Jadwiga patted her grandson's hand still sitting on her shoulder. "My days of fighting the *Sensu* are over." Looking back at Deena, she added, "Do not fear, for I know you will find the strength you need. We have done everything necessary—protected everyone we needed to protect. We—"

Deena suddenly sat up. *Oh, my God.* She bolted from the couch. *How could I have left her out?*

"What is it, Deena?" said Simon.

"It's Maggie. I forgot Maggie Doherty. She'll never survive an attack. I need to bring her here."

Jadwiga sat upright. "Get her and come back quickly!"

Deena ran for the door.

"Wait for me!" said Simon.

They reached the car, Deena in the lead, Simon following. He took the wheel and they careened down the street toward Wilshire.

If anything happened to Maggie, Deena would never forgive herself. What had she been thinking, not including her as someone she cared for?

"Listen to me," said Deena. "Once Maggie's protection has been taken care of and I get some final instructions, I want you to stay with everyone while I go back to our house alone."

"What? Why?"

"The *Sensu* is coming for me, and I won't have you all get caught in the crossfire—whatever that may be."

"There's no way I'm letting you do that."

"I'm not going to fight about this. You need to stay with Jadwiga."

Simon stared out at the road, holding the steering wheel in his tight fists. "We'll talk about it when we get back."

"But—"

"I said, we'll talk about it," said Simon, raising his voice.

Deena decided to let it go, for now. But she knew exactly what was going to happen. Simon would be staying at Jadwiga's.

They sped into the Wilshire lot, parked the car, and ran into the lobby.

"Hey!" yelled a voice. "You need to sign in!"

They ignored the woman behind the counter, bypassed the elevator, and ran up the stairs to the second floor. Deena prayed it wasn't too late.

When they stepped into Maggie's room, she stopped dead.

The bed was stripped. The get-well cards on the walls had been taken down. There were no flowers on the bureau, and the closet stood open and empty.

"Oh, Deena," said Simon. "I'm so sorry."

She ran from the room to the nurses' station, Simon in tow.

"What happened to Maggie Doherty?" she asked.

The nurse looked at her, puzzled. "Who?"

"Maggie Doherty, my aunt's friend." When the nurse stared back, Deena added, "For God's sake, she's a patient here! She was in the room to the left of my aunt."

The nurse tilted her head. "That room has been empty since before your aunt arrived."

Deena staggered.

Empty? She couldn't have imagined her, could she?

She brushed past Simon, ignoring the look on his face. He'd never met Maggie. He'd only heard about her through Deena.

But she seemed so real.

Deena replayed their conversations over the last two months.

Had Maggie been alone that first time they'd met? Deena remembered the smile on her face as she walked down the hall with her walker.

Care to dance?

All those sayings of hers.

As I say to my children ...

Every conversation.

I'm sure your aunt loves you very much.

Deena searched her memory, looking for one time—just one—when someone else had been around when they spoke.

No.

Tried to remember if she'd ever asked the staff about Maggie.

No.

Had Deena *ever* seen a single person other than herself speaking to Maggie?

Only one.

Agatha.

Then she remembered.

I have five children—each more special than the last.

Five children.

Five.

Deena sprinted toward her aunt's room. It couldn't be true. She loved Maggie. She would force Agatha to tell her the truth.

"Wait for me," called Simon.

"I don't want you to come. There's no telling what I'll find."

"Like I'd really let you go alone."

He reached for her hand, and for the briefest of seconds she thought of batting it away. He shouldn't be there; it wasn't safe. But while Deena had talked a good game, now that she was in it, she wasn't sure she could go on alone. She took his hand. She had to.

They burst into Agatha's room and found her asleep, wearing a contented look on her lined face. Deena grabbed her by the shoulders and shook, but her aunt just lay there.

"My, my," said a voice from behind. "If it isn't Deena and Simple Simon. Nice of you to come."

Deena spun toward the door. "Maggie?"

And it *was* Maggie . . . with a difference. She stood up straight. Her eyes were slightly slanted, her smile smug and superior. There was something about her hands that gave Deena a chill. A subtle ripple under the skin, as if Maggie was flexing, getting ready to lash out, to squeeze, to grab. It screamed danger. The kind you sense when you pass a dark alley or empty building—a danger that lies in wait, quiet and focused. And there was a sound . . . a low rumbling coming from Maggie's chest.

Purring.

Simon placed himself in front of Deena. "So you're Maggie. I've heard a lot about you, but I have to say, I imagined someone quite different."

Damn it, thought Deena. *He doesn't have a clue what he's dealing with.*

Simon stood there as if he could stop whatever happened next.

She grabbed his shoulder and squeezed.

"Funny. You're exactly what I expected," said Maggie with a smooth, controlled hum. "A silly little man with the delusion that he can make a difference."

"What, exactly, are you?" demanded Deena, hoping to take Maggie's attention away from Simon.

Maggie closed the door with a simple wave of her hand. "Didn't my old friend, Jadwiga, tell you?"

"You—you're the *Sensu*? But I thought—"

"You thought I was an invisible entity living in a netherworld, pulling strings from afar." Maggie chuckled. "Jadwiga has believed that for sixty years. I enjoy coming onto this plane from time to time, something Jadwiga has never known. I'm here now because over the years, she has caused quite a bit of damage. It's time I take care of it in person."

A deep sigh suddenly came from Agatha, still lying asleep on the bed. The slight smile on her aunt's lips triggered Deena's growing hatred for her. All this—the danger, the pain—had started with Agatha, and yet, there she lay, with a smile on her face. It took all of Deena's self-control to stop from slapping it away.

"I wouldn't concern yourself with your aunt," Maggie said, smoothly. "Agatha is having another one of her dreams—a visit to the forest she created." She glided to the foot of the bed and looked down at Agatha with amusement. "It's where she goes to, let's say, recharge. After your young friend's tussle with *Visu*, there's a lot to absorb. But you know all about Agatha's sanctuary. I believe you had the pleasure of visiting it not too long ago."

Deena had been there, all right. At the time she'd thought it was a nightmare. The forest and the lake and those frightening objects floating in the water. It had been that nightmare and Agatha's voice whispering *Ready or not . . . here I come*, that had been the beginning of it all.

She felt Simon grab her by the shoulder and drag her toward the door. He wrenched it open and they ran out into the hallway with the *Sensu*'s parting words following close behind.

"Run, little mouse. Run."

30

Deena's relief at getting out of the room was short-lived.

When she and Simon stepped into the hallway, they found the second floor empty—of people, anyway.

"What the hell is this?" said Simon.

The chairs, the nurses' station, the structural pillars—they were being overrun by a growing forest encroaching on every surface. The linoleum floor was disintegrating, turning into a dirt path that led down the hall to a lake in the distance. There were loud cracking sounds as plants here and there broke through the ground in their search for light and air. Vines slithered up the walls. Unidentifiable creatures could be heard scurrying in the undergrowth, making ominous chittering noises. The light was gradually fading, swallowed up by a forest alive with danger.

Simon released his grip on Deena's arm and propped himself against the wall for support. He didn't notice the tangle of vines slowly snaking along the floor toward where he stood.

Deena turned her head just as the first coil twisted around his leg.

"Simon, move!"

He looked down and yelled, "Get it off!"

Deena reached him in two steps and together they grabbed hold of the tough husk. It writhed in their hands and cut into their palms as they struggled to break Simon free. With an audible snap, the branch finally broke in two with the vine's screams of pain shuddering down the hall, its blood, thick and brown, seeping from its ragged ends.

"Let's get out of here!" cried Deena as she grabbed Simon's hand.

They ran down the corridor toward the stairwell. As they did, the walls grew thick with the clinging branches and leaves of a hedgerow. Deena watched them closely for fear they may get trapped within the branches' tendrils—which was when she noticed the faces deep within their shadows.

These weren't just plants. These were people, imprisoned by the *Sensu*—their faces frozen in torment, their mouths thrown open in pain, their eyes haunted with past deeds, their hands reaching out for salvation.

This was Agatha's destiny—the price she would pay for the *Sensu*'s gifts.

Up ahead was the stairwell. Deena had no idea what they'd find when they opened that door, but it was their only way out.

One step at a time. Get to the lobby. Out to the car. Back to Jadwiga's, and safety.

It looked as if they were going to make it.

Nearly there.

And then, thank God, they reached the door.

Simon grabbed the doorknob and pulled.

A creeping cold blew up from the stairwell, followed by thick mist gathering at the top landing, cutting them off. The mist consolidated into a figure with a barely discernible head and limbs. Its movements were sinuous, amorphous, constantly changing. Sparks of light surrounded it, crackling the air, depositing a rotten-egg stench of sulfur.

The only recognizable feature was a face slowly emerging from deep within. Maggie's face, laughing.

It pushed them back into the hall and slammed the door. The face came in and out of focus as the figure grew in height, reaching the ceiling and blocking their path. It then unhinged its jaw and from its mouth an avalanche of water flooded the corridor.

Deena tumbled end over end, losing any sense of up or down. She needed air. And my God, where was Simon?

She felt his hand latch onto her wrist. Together they were tossed like so much flotsam in an angry sea. They struggled toward the light, but their ankles and legs were tangled in the branches of an underwater plant that threatened to pull them down. Simon managed to kick himself free and helped tear the plants off Deena. With the last of their air they swam to the surface and broke through, gasping.

The water suddenly receded and they were left lying in the mud back at Agatha's door, drenched and shivering.

The *Sensu's* voice crept into Deena's head.

"By all means, try again," it purred. "I relish the waves of panic wafting off your bodies. It reminds me of the enticing aroma of freshly baked bread."

"Jesus," said Simon catching his breath. "It's playing with us."

Deena crawled over to Simon and they huddled together on the floor, desperate for warmth. He was in danger now because of her.

"I never wanted you in the middle of this," she said.

"What? You would deprive me of all the fun?" Simon turned her face toward his and, as if it was just another day, gave Deena a long kiss.

"Just in case . . ." he whispered.

She blinked away the mist gathering in her eyes. Now was not the time.

"If we can break the *Sensu's* connection to Agatha, it might help," she whispered.

"What if Agatha was dead? Would that work?"

"I think so." Deena suddenly remembered the promise she'd made to herself back at Silver Lake: If her aunt didn't die on her own, Deena would do the honors.

Big talk. No guts.

Fact was, Deena didn't have it in her.

Simon could read the hesitation on her face. He raised her chin so that their eyes met and, with their faces inches apart, pointed to himself.

Simon would do it. That made sense. The *Sensu* was so focused on Deena, she might be able to distract it while Simon did the deed. But how?

Simon must have seen the doubt in her eyes. He took his open hands, palms up, and raised them toward his face.

A pillow. He'd use a pillow.

With a flurry of hand signals, it was decided that she would stay in the hall and engage the *Sensu* in conversation, an argument, a negotiation, something.

Simon dug into the still-wet earth and brought together a mound of mud. He took off his shirt and draped it over the mound, fashioning a rough approximation of a body lying on the ground. He then opened the door to Agatha's room just wide enough to slip in.

When the door clicked shut, Deena turned back around and yelled, "Hey! I wanna talk to you!"

A biting wind cut into Deena's face as the *Sensu* materialized. The person she had known as Maggie was gone. In her place was a formless creature, coming in and out of focus with those same sparks of light firing around it.

"I would love to have a conversation with you, my dear. What's on your mind?"

"I wanna make a deal."

"Oh?"

"Leave my husband and friends alone and I'll bring you Jadwiga. That's who you really want, right?"

The *Sensu* sneered. "I don't need *you* to bring Jadwiga to me."

"No? If you could have gotten her on your own, you would have done it by now. She's protected herself. My guess is that you need a conduit. And that conduit has to bring Jadwiga physically close."

The figure grew darker.

Deena smiled. "I can see I'm right. Your primary connection is with my aunt. She's the key. Through her you've reached me, and through me you've reached Kayla. It's like a chain. The only way to one is through another. You need someone directly connected to my aunt to bring Jadwiga to you."

"You know nothing," the *Sensu* whispered, blowing past Deena and crashing through Agatha's door.

Deena saw Simon standing over her aunt with the full weight of his body pushing a pillow down on her face. There was no hatred or grim determination on his face. Instead, he looked down at Agatha with his head pulled back in fear, as if he was being forced to watch someone else do the suffocating.

Sparks of light in an angry shade of red flew off the *Sensu* as it wrapped itself around Simon's body. He grabbed ahold of the sheet and then the bed frame, trying to stop himself from being dragged away. But it was no good. The *Sensu* had him.

"Simon!" Deena tried to run into the room, but the Sensu slammed her against the opposite wall of the hallway. Deena scrambled back up and got to the open door, helplessly watching as Simon was whipped from one end of the room to the other, his body jerking grotesquely with each new direction. His head lurched from side to side. His arms thrashed. His legs wrenched this way and that as the *Sensu* flung him against the walls, over and over again.

"Let him go! I'm the one you want!"

The *Sensu's* voice whispered gently in her head. "Be patient, my lovely. Your time is nearly here."

31

Everything suddenly changed.

There was no Agatha lying in a hospital bed. And there was no Simon.

Deena was sitting in an armchair pulled up to a round table in an all-white room—chairs, table, walls, floors, ceiling, everything. Her eyes stung from the brightness of it.

She prayed Simon was alive, but she knew that surviving the thrashing he'd received was too much to hope for. She desperately wanted to search for him, but her arms and legs were somehow bound to the chair.

She should have stopped him from following her into Agatha's room. She should have forced him to go back to Jadwiga's. That's what people do when they love someone. Protect them.

Jadwiga was wrong. Deena was incapable of love.

Hanging above the table was a slowly spinning carcass under which a bucket had been placed to catch drips of blood. It was the body of a person, but its back was turned. Deena couldn't see who it was. If only she could get out of the chair—and yet she knew she would fail at even that. She had lost everything before the battle had even begun.

A single trail of blood traveled down the carcass's dirty ankle and headed toward the big toe, where it hesitated for a moment before plopping into the waiting bucket. Then the carcass turned, showing the chest split open and the ribs spread apart like the doors of an open gate laying the backbone bare.

Deena didn't want to look at the face, but her eyes, as if on their own, traveled up past the gaping chest.

It was Jadwiga. Her wrinkles were cut deeply into her skin like the creases of an old crumpled bag. The droop of her mouth was now so pronounced, it looked as if her face was melting.

And then the carcass changed. It became her mother's body, rotted away by cancer; her right cheek gone, exposing the teeth within. Her eyes, empty sockets. Her hair, sparse and brittle.

It wasn't her mother.

Now it was Deena with hard, dead eyes staring at nothing. A stone face with no expression, no compassion. A mouth set in a cruel line.

Jadwiga.

Mother.

Deena.

The face changed faster and faster until the whole body suddenly became Simon, battered and broken by the *Sensu*. Deena thought that what she was seeing was an illusion, but she couldn't be sure. She couldn't even be sure if Simon had been hurt in Agatha's room. She couldn't be sure of anything.

She wanted to get up out of her chair and cut Simon down. She wanted to lay him on the floor so she could bandage his wounds. But all she could do was watch helplessly as her husband hung from a hook. Blood flowed from a deep crevice in his skull, exposing his brain, torn and pulsing. A jagged rib had pierced through his chest. Half his nose had been torn away, leaving raw, mangled flesh in its place.

He lifted his hand toward Deena, his eyes begging for help. Then with a loud cry he burst into flame, incinerating into black ash that fell into a pile on the table. A breeze suddenly picked up, gathering the ash into its eddy and carrying it away.

"Simon!"

And just like that, she understood that she was alone.

Deena sat in the bright whiteness, unable to move. She desperately needed to know if Simon was alive.

After what seemed an eternity, a figure—blurred at first—appeared to her right. It was the *Sensu* wearing Maggie's body. It brought its face close to Deena's neck and breathed in deeply.

"Mmm. Lovely." It then stepped back and regarded Deena with amusement. "What an entertaining time we've had."

"Where's Simon?" demanded Deena.

"Ah, Simon. I find it amusing that you believed you could kill your aunt without my knowledge—that I wouldn't sense your husband fashioning a pathetic decoy from a pile of mud. This is my domain. I thought that was obvious." The *Sensu* combed its hand through Deena's hair, its fingers dragging against her scalp. "Don't misunderstand. That is exactly the type of initiative I appreciate. It's too bad it must end."

Deena's teeth ground together as she tried to pull away. "You haven't answered my question. Tell me where my husband is."

"Your tenacity is touching, but I can't be bothered keeping track of these sorts of things. Whatever happened, happened."

If Deena could have moved, she would have been on her feet with her hands around the *Sensu's* throat. But her invisible bonds made that impossible. She threw back her head and let out a scream of anger and frustration. Then, breathless, she stared at the *Sensu* and said, "I swear to God, I will find a way to stop you."

The *Sensu* laughed. "Charming. But we still have plenty on the menu to sample."

It stepped back and regarded Deena with interest.

"I suspect you've had quite a time with Jadwiga. You should have seen her when she was young. Such a formidable opponent. While Jadwiga's power may be coming to an end, she will still be one of my greatest acquisitions. I just need to dispatch the parts that she has scattered here and there. Once that's done, Jadwiga will belong to me."

"Parts?"

The *Sensu* came closer. "Yesss." It pressed its index finger to Deena's left temple. "Parts." Its pointed fingernail bit into Deena's skin as it traveled down her face, past her ear, and toward her chin, scratching the surface just enough to cause a shiver of pain.

Deena held her breath, refusing to give it the satisfaction of crying out.

The *Sensu* brought its lips to Deena's ear and in a lover's whisper said, "Do you still feel her?" The heat of its breath moved like a bellows in and out, in and out. "I'm sure you do, but not for long. Once Agatha has entered into your body, you will be the bridge that brings Jadwiga to me."

A shudder traveled down Deena's arms and spread into her hands at the prospect of losing herself to Agatha.

The *Sensu* straightened up, took a step back, and said, "The time has come for *Tactu*. No one can deny the sensation of touch, but when it's accompanied by its brothers . . . *that's* where reality truly resides."

Deena answered with a belligerence that surprised even her. "I've already experienced four of your little helpers, and I'm a helluva lot stronger because of it. Go ahead. Bring it."

The *Sensu* laughed. "And how did your newfound strength help your husband?"

Deena's blood rushed to her face. She strained to break free even though she knew it was useless. But she was wrong. Her right arm suddenly jerked up. Her eyes darted from her hand to the *Sensu's* face just in time to see it change from amusement to curiosity. With a flick of the *Sensu's* wrist, Deena's hand was bound to the chair once again.

"Well, now, aren't you full of surprises." It walked around the chair, dragging its hand along Deena's shoulders. "It would appear there's more to you than meets the eye. Perhaps I should give you the opportunity to face your enemy fairly."

"What the hell are you talking about?"

"My dear, have you never wondered who Agatha truly is? What she has actually done?"

"I know exactly who she is. I also know that you've twisted her into someone she was never meant to be."

"Deena, please. I never change the bedrock of a person's true nature. I optimize their basic self. Answer their call. Provide them with tools. There are things you don't know about Agatha—ways she has affected your life."

Deena held her breath, waiting for more. The *Sensu* was offering what she wanted most: knowledge and clarity. She wanted to know what had happened between her mother and Agatha. She wanted to understand the connection she had with her aunt. But most of all, she wanted to know why Agatha hated Deena so much that she'd offer her up as a sacrifice. Did the *Sensu* have answers, or was Deena being played?

The *Sensu*'s voice grew softer, kinder. "I see that you have questions, and honestly, my dear, I would be happy to answer them. But you need to ask me. I need to hear the request from your own lips."

Deena didn't know what to do. Yes, she needed answers, but if the *Sensu* was offering to help, she should surely say no. And yet, Deena had to have this—had to see who Agatha was. This was her moment to discover everything.

"I can smell your curiosity," said the *Sensu*. "It fills the room like a field of lilacs in full bloom. Let me make it easy for you. Just say the word, Deena. Say yes. That's all that's needed. One word. *Yes*."

The pressure in Deena's head made it difficult to think. A little knowledge wouldn't do any harm. She wanted—no, she *needed* this.

She set her jaw and averted her eyes as she breathed a quiet "Yes."

And instantly a swirl of wind wound around them, growing faster and more powerful. With each turn Deena was presented with a different image from her past.

There she was as a friendless preteen, reading in her room.

And then a toddler too frightened to climb onto her trike.

And then a baby held at her mother's breast.

The images scrolled faster and faster, growing smaller and smaller, until Deena's life slid into darkness as a new scene emerged.

A nineteen-year-old Agatha sat in a diner processing the unimaginable.

How could you? How could you? I would have gone through fire for you.

The love of Agatha's life and her twenty-four-year-old sister had conspired behind her back.

I'll never forgive you. You can both burn in hell!

Deena could never have imagined her parents capable of such a thing. She felt Agatha's devastation as keenly as if it were her own.

And there was more.

A struggling Agatha made her way in New York, bearing rejection after rejection, proving that she was "less than," destined to be alone. Deena saw the cruel way Michael had treated her, and that betrayal set the pattern for the next man, and the next. The man who cheated on her with her friend. The one who stole her jewelry. The one who got her pregnant and ran. Agatha was soon hardened by it, even as her insides grew stooped from the weight of her pain.

With each new memory Deena got closer to a billowing red curtain drawn across a stage. When it was just a few feet away her mother crossed in front of the curtain, looking at Deena, desperately trying to speak. She shook her head and waved her hands as if to say, *Close your eyes. This is not for you.*

But Zahra didn't see the oily black figure crawling out from beneath the curtain. It inched closer to where she stood and then rose to double in size. Its bear-shaped form wrapped itself around Zahra and squeezed. She fought to get free with a growing panic taking over her face, but she wasn't strong enough. With Zahra now trapped inside, the creature grew smaller, until all that was left was a dime-size spot dripping off the stage and out of sight.

A blanket of quiet fell over the room, broken finally by the sound of footsteps. The *Sensu* in the form of Maggie calmly entered from stage left and stood proudly in front of the curtain.

"You wanted answers." It dramatically raised its arm and, with an impresario's flick of the hand, parted the curtain.

A round of phantom applause cracked the air.

"Then answers you shall have."

32

Deena found herself in an all-too-familiar setting. A stage.

She was standing on the doorstep of a facade that had been built to look like the house she'd grown up in. The applause was for her—the star's entrance. She squinted to see the audience past the blinding footlights, but all she could make out was a wall of darkness. Deena turned back toward the set piece and rang the bell.

Her father opened the door and stood for a moment, stooped and graying and just a little fragile. He was smaller than she remembered, and it pulled at her heart. But mixed with that poignancy was her excitement at seeing him again. Nabil had died without an opportunity for her to say good-bye. This may well have been an illusion, but Deena still welcomed the chance to share a few last words with him. She reached out for a hug but was unable to move. She couldn't even manage to call out his name.

Surprise registered on her father's face at the sight of her, but it quickly gave way to resignation. "Hello, Aggie. Come in."

Aggie? thought Deena.

"That's right, my dear," came the *Sensu's* voice. *"You are inside your aunt. Your answers, as promised, are about to be delivered."*

Agatha followed Nabil into the house while Deena tried to get her bearings. It was surprising to see that her aunt had visited her parents. Except for attending her parents' funerals, she hadn't been to Philadelphia in years.

To the left was the small couch and marble coffee table that had held pride of place for as long as she could remember. Next to it was a recliner and folding TV table holding the remnants of Nabil's lunch. Across from the recliner was a television on a metal stand tuned to the local news.

It was the picture of her mother on the end table flanked by an arrangement of wilted flowers that told Deena when this was taking place. Both had come from her mother's funeral back in 1979. Deena had stayed with her father for all of a week after the service was over, leaving him to face his sorrow alone—one of the many unforgivable things she had done. The dead flowers told Deena that she had already left. Nabil didn't have long to live.

There she stood, a few feet away from her father, with the possibility of forgiveness dangling in front of her and no way to grasp it.

Nabil turned off the television and cleared away his lunch while Agatha made herself comfortable on the couch. When he came back, he took a seat on the recliner.

"So, what brings you back so soon after the funeral, Aggie?"

"Nothing much. I thought it would be nice to visit. How are you holding up?"

Nabil sat back and crossed his legs. "You came all the way from New York. For a visit."

"Of course I did. You're my brother-in-law."

Nabil smiled and looked down. "Well, well . . . how about that."

Deena recognized her father's narrowed eyes and tucked-in chin. It was the look he wore to hide disappointment or anger, but Agatha didn't seem to notice.

"Y'know, Nabil, we've had twenty-five years of difficulty, you and I. Maybe the time has come to put those years behind us."

"Yes. I suppose you could say we had difficulty."

"I just want you to know I forgive you."

Nabil rubbed the back of his neck. "Hmmph. Interesting." He sat in his recliner, nodding as he stared at the space in front of him. Then he tilted his head to one side, raised his eyes to Agatha, and said, "Where was your forgiveness when Zahra was sick?"

"Excuse me?"

"Not a visit—not a phone call. But I get it. Pancreatic cancer isn't pretty."

"What exactly are you saying?"

"Where were you, Aggie? Huh? And what about Deena? You kept her away until the very end. Zahra was denied the company of her own daughter during the worst of her illness."

Deena flinched at the sound of her name. The guilt she had lived with did more than find its mark. Her father's words magnified the weight of everything Deena had been carrying.

He was winding up now—leaning forward in his seat with his hands on his knees, the vein on the left side of his temple swelling. Deena watched through Agatha's eyes as he said, "Zahra died with no peace in her heart. She was tortured right up to the end."

All because of what I did, thought Deena. She wanted to run away, to hide her face, but that wouldn't stop her father's voice from following her wherever she went.

"Zahra was tortured?" said Agatha. "What about me?"

"She had cancer! What in God's name are you talking about?"

"I've had a lifetime of torture. No husband. No family. When is it supposed to be my turn?"

"What is wrong with you? Zahra was your sister. And you were nineteen years old. People move on."

"You *would* think that, wouldn't you!" she said with growing anger. "You have no idea what the last twenty-five years of my life has been like—what you and Zahra turned me into." Agatha thrust herself forward. "I have nothing!"

"That was your choice."

"No! You made that choice for me. You and Zahra. I must be the stupidest woman on the planet to think you'd want to be with me now that Zahra is gone."

Nabil's face twisted in revulsion. "Be with *you*? Is that why you're here?" He gave a small laugh at the thought. "I never wanted to be with you."

The room darkened and the air cooled as a translucent image of her mother appeared next to her father and placed a hand on his shoulder in an effort to stop him from speaking. He couldn't see her. He didn't even know she was there.

Something terrible was about to happen.

Nabil looked at the shocked expression on Agatha's face and drove the point home.

"Not clear enough for you, Aggie? Let me put it this way." He lowered his head and spoke slowly and clearly. "You were nothing to me."

"But . . . we were together," she insisted.

Nabil let out a quiet laugh. "You *are* the stupidest woman on the planet. In what world would anyone want you when Zahra Haddad was in the room? I fell in love the minute I laid eyes on her. You were simply a path to the greatest love of my life."

Deena felt Agatha's muscles coil as she nearly came out of her seat. "You son of a bitch! You ruined my life! Look at you, sitting in your suburban dump, mourning the loss of your precious Zahra. Well, let me tell you something: You may have had Zahra, but you won't have Deena."

"What?"

"Deena is mine," she said, her head thrown back in triumph, "and I have plans that will make my ruined life look like a church picnic compared to what's in store for her."

A translucent Zahra ran to Agatha and knelt down. She tried to grab her hand, tried to speak to her, but failed again.

Nabil grew pale as he clutched the arms of the recliner.

Her aunt's words were too much for her father to take. Deena screamed for Agatha to stop, but it didn't work.

"Are you scared, Nabil?" sneered Agatha. "Worried for your little Deena? Well, you should be!"

"I—I'll stop you. She'll listen to me. I'll tell her everything."

Agatha laughed. "And what will you tell her? That you and her sainted mother stabbed me in the back? How will little Deena feel about that?"

He should have told me, thought Deena, with her fear mounting at the unfolding scene. *I would have understood.*

"Please, Aggie." Nabil was struggling for air. "She's all I have left."

"And what do *I* have? I'll tell you. I have Deena. She belongs to me. I will destroy her life the way you destroyed mine."

What does she mean by that? What had Agatha done?

Deena saw her father grab his chest as he pointed to a bottle of pills on top of the television.

"My pills," he said. "I need my pills."

Deena desperately tried to make Agatha move. Her father was in trouble and her aunt needed to get him those pills.

It must have worked, because Agatha turned toward the television. But, my God, she was moving so slowly.

"*Hurry!*" screamed Deena. She wanted to burst out of Agatha's skin and grab the pills herself.

Agatha finally reached the television, picked up the pills, and turned back toward Nabil.

Okay, thought Deena. *Now get them to my father.*

But Agatha just stood there as she regarded Nabil with an almost clinical curiosity.

"Bring it here," Nabil croaked. "Quickly."

Deena saw the vision of her mother sitting on the edge of the couch with her head thrust forward and her tightly held fists buried in her lap.

Agatha finally started walking toward Nabil as he extended his arm with an open hand, hoping to grab the medicine more quickly. But her leisurely pace made it clear that she was enjoying every second.

Nabil rose from his seat, his legs shaking, barely able to hold him up. Then his eyes, shocked and betrayed, suddenly locked onto Agatha's as he pitched forward with all the weight of a falling tree, hitting his temple on the edge of the marble coffee table with an audible crack. His head jerked back and his body crashed to the floor where he lay on his side—the blood, thick and dark, pooling under his head.

"*Papa!*" screamed Deena.

The force of her scream twisted around her waist and propelled her out of Agatha's body and into a wind tunnel, where she tumbled end over end, barely able to breathe.

When it finally stopped, Deena found herself back in the white room sitting in a chair in front of the stage, an audience of one. The last of her scream faded away until all that was left was an anticipatory hum vibrating just below the surface.

Deena watched as Agatha stood there with her hands tightly clasped in front of her, as if she were trying to hold her body together. She whispered, "What have I done?" She moved a step closer. "Nabil?"

No answer.

"Nabil!"

She knelt down and put her hand under Nabil's nose. With a quiet gasp she quickly stood and backed into the couch, never once taking her eyes off of Nabil. He looked back at her with an accusatory stare.

And there was blood. So much blood.

Agatha wrapped her arms around her body and rocked back and forth. Her mouth opened wide and an animal-like sound escaped her lips. It started as a lament, low and wretched. Then it grew louder and higher in a horrible crescendo. She threw back her head and let out a wail as deep and wide and long as the village mourners' keening for the dead, screaming at heaven, screaming at hell.

Black clouds closed in on Agatha, spiraling around her body, moving from her waist to her breasts to her throat to her face. Her mouth opened even wider, but this time it was as if it was being forced. The smoke, like a snake, uncoiled and entered into her mouth, her eyes growing wide as she stared up at the ceiling. Her arms, torso, and legs shook violently in a macabre dance with her head thrown back and her throat making rapid-fire gagging sounds. The whoosh of air grew louder as the smoke forced itself into her mouth, the last of it disappearing with a final groan like a whirl of water disappearing down a drain.

When the smoke was gone—when it had forced itself into her— the hum abruptly stopped and an unnatural quiet weighed the air down. Agatha stopped shaking. Her mouth and eyes were closed. She calmly sat on the couch wearing a slight smile, showing neither worry nor fear. And when her eyelids lifted, her eyes were staring ahead, transformed into two pitch-black orbs.

She calmly stood, brushed a wrinkle from her skirt, pushed a lock of hair into place, and without a look in Nabil's direction, slowly walked out the door.

And bravos punched the air as an unseen audience burst into applause.

33

Deena's anger started small, a knot in her chest, expanding up into her throat and then her head, rising like a monster reeking with the moist hot steam of rage. It pressed against the back of her eyes as her breathing stoked the heat until she could contain it no longer.

She screamed. Her balled-up fists were squeezed so tightly that her nails drew blood in the palms of her hands, her stigmata of rage.

"She killed him!"

The years of deference and respect she had wasted on her father's murderer made her want to tear out her own hair. Her cry of outrage was so deep and strong that her arms and legs broke free from their invisible bonds.

She jumped from her seat and paced the floor. "Damn her!" she yelled. "Damn her!"

Deena had spent years burdened with guilt and self-hatred over her father's lonely death. And all along it had been Agatha, Agatha, Agatha.

The *Sensu* stood in a dark corner watching with what looked like compassion in its eyes.

"It is so very unfair, don't you think?" it said gently. "It was not your fault that you were conceived from a union of betrayal. It was not your fault that that union tied you to Agatha, a woman capable of killing a person who was not only your father, but the man she loved."

That's true. Why was I the one saddled with her care?

"And yes, your parents changed the course of Agatha's life by that betrayal, but it doesn't excuse what Agatha did."

It doesn't. There is no justification for murder.

"And when I think of how you cared for her, while all along she held this dreadful secret. It's just too much."

She never appreciated it. She never appreciated me, *after all I did.*

"I have seen so many like you who were treated unfairly, but it is within your power to balance the scales."

The scales must *be balanced. She shouldn't be allowed to get away with it.*

"And all you need do is ask."

Deena stopped.

She turned toward the *Sensu* as sweat ran down her reddened face, and in a voice rubbed raw with anger, whispered, "How?"

The *Sensu* glided toward Deena, now standing in the middle of the white room, and gently placed its hand on her shoulder. Deena felt the heat of its touch travel down toward her stomach where it burrowed, bubbling and churning.

"I was wrong about you, Deena, and that doesn't happen often. I can see you have the courage to right a terrible wrong. I can help."

"You can?" Deena stared at the *Sensu*'s eyes. *Such beautiful eyes.*

"Of course I can. Let me ask. What is the penalty for murder?"

"Death."

And its eyes are filled with understanding and compassion.

"Yes, Deena, death. And there is no better person to mete out that punishment than the daughter of the murdered man." The *Sensu*

223

stroked Deena's cheek, pushing the sound of her voice deep into the center of her consciousness.

It understands me. I'm safe.

With a wave of its arm, plants broke through the floor along the edges of the room, growing into thick bushes. Trees inched up toward the ceiling as the air grew thick and heavy. Agatha lay asleep in the midst of this growing forest, like a blameless tourist in the very nightmare she had created.

Deena breathed in the humid air, and with each breath her connection to the *Sensu* grew. The surrounding plants did more than clear her mind. They nurtured the rage that seeped out from her pores, allowing it to rise up and encircle her face. Everything she saw and everything she heard was through the lens of her anger.

The *Sensu* placed its hands on Deena's shoulders, turned her toward Agatha, and quietly stepped back.

"Do this for your father," it whispered. "It's time for him to find peace."

Deena's body coiled inward and then propelled her to the bed where she snatched up Agatha's pillow.

She's a murderer. She deserves to die.

As Deena brought the pillow down, Agatha's arms came alive, blocking its path. A muffled voice from underneath cried, "Deena, no!"

Agatha's voice only spurred her on. Deena placed her left knee on the edge of the bed for leverage while her aunt took hold of the pillow with both hands and thrashed in panic. Her screams, like the bleating of a sacrificial goat, filled the room until Agatha managed to pull the pillow away just enough for her eyes to become visible.

Those eyes—holding Deena in place as they looked up at her with the same panic her father had shown to Agatha just before he died.

Deena felt a jolt.

She suddenly noticed where she was standing, felt the pillow she was holding.

My God. What am I doing?

Agatha whimpered, "Please, Deena, stop."

"Don't listen to her," yelled the *Sensu*. "Your father deserves justice."

Deena shook her head from side to side, trying to clear away the stranglehold of black thoughts that had taken control of who she was. Her breathing slowed as she lowered her hands.

And quiet descended onto the room.

"You ..." sneered the *Sensu*. "You are nothing but a weak, pathetic excuse for a human being. I offer you a path toward freedom and you don't have the courage to take it."

"I won't become the evil thing you turned my aunt into." Deena flung the pillow across the room. "You can go to hell."

"I see," the *Sensu* answered. "You think you're blameless. You think you're good. After *Tactu* is through with you, you will know exactly what you are."

The *Sensu* grabbed hold of Deena's face, bringing with it a smell of musk so overpowering, she was afraid to breathe. The harder Deena tried to pull away, the tighter the *Sensu's* fingers dug into her flesh.

"I'll have you, with or without your compliance. If you had completed your task, I would have given you thirty years of life. With that task left undone, my children will devour you until there is nothing left but an empty husk. You will finally have the pleasure of meeting *Tactu*."

The *Sensu* grabbed Deena by the hair and dragged her into a chair. It then stood in the middle of the room and, like the conductor of a great orchestra, coaxed the trees along the edges to rise upward until their branches wove into a thick canopy. The walls fell away, revealing a wide vista where ferns and moss off in the distance crept toward Deena, creating a winding path to a dark lake, black and ominous, now forming at her feet.

Deena suddenly realized that she was sitting in the middle of the very nightmare that had started it all. Even though it had happened months ago, it was still fresh in her mind. Her mother had been in it. And so had Agatha.

Ready or not . . . here I come.

The thicker the trees grew, the darker it became, until that darkness pressed against Deena's eyes. She tried to find a pinprick of light in the hope that it would stop the panic, but there was none. She struggled for air as her chest squeezed the breath out of her, until, thank God, a faint light glowed in the distance. She hungrily grabbed hold of it as it undulated into the shape of a figure.

It was her mother, standing expressionless, unaware of Deena's presence, and it calmed her.

But then Zahra grew thin, her face became gaunt, and her hair fell away in clumps. Bit by bit she turned into the burden of memories Deena had lived with for years. She watched in real time as her mother rotted away.

It's not my mother. It's Visu.

And Deena understood all too keenly that what she had dreaded most had finally begun.

34

Zahra stood motionless in the distance, her lips pulled back in a rictus smile with teeth blackened and skin draped over her bones like a decomposing animal's hide.

Deena steadied herself on the chair, remembering how she had battled *Visu* the first time. If she held onto the knowledge that the vision wasn't real, it would eventually go away. She had done it once. She could do it again.

When Zahra spied Deena she suddenly came to life. Her face craned forward and her grin curled into an angry mask. "You," she rasped. "I bore you. Suckled you. Loved you. And at my most fragile, at the point of my greatest need, you abandoned me."

"But it wasn't me," said Deena, still holding on. "It was Aunt Agatha, pulling the strings."

"Not true," said Zahra. "My life was moldering away . . . I was in my own private hell while you were living *this*."

Zahra stepped onto the moss-covered path with a grotesque marionette's gait and made her way around the lake until she stood in front of Deena with her face just inches away. Reflected in Zahra's eyes were twin images of Deena sitting in her Manhattan apartment, laughing with friends and enjoying a meal, while her mother's body was being eaten away by the acid touch of cancer.

Deena cried, "But I'm a good person!"

"Not even close," spat out Zahra. "You doubled my sorrow as I waited day after day and week after week for you to come."

"I didn't know," said Deena. "I didn't—"

"Liar!" Zahra's voice was thick with hatred. A sound mimicking laughter came from her blackened mouth as she lowered her head and, in a high-pitched singsong voice, said, "A daughter must never abandon her family. Isn't that right, Dolly-Deena?" Her voice changed to a shriek. "But you! You built family loyalty into a cathedral and then destroyed it stone by stone, leaving me to rot in the rubble."

I—I'm sorry, thought Deena weakly.

"I will come to you in your dreams until it becomes so unbearable you will want to die." Zahra threw her head back and let out a ragged yowl. "But I won't allow your death. You will live a long life, tormented by your actions. Every look in the mirror will reveal what you really are."

A mirror appeared in front of Deena, and she took in an aching breath at what she saw: a Dorian Gray–like vision of her selfishness, made manifest—stooped and twisted, with eyes hardened by cold-blooded indifference.

It was more than she could bear.

"Please," cried Deena. "Take it away."

Zahra bent down and brought her cracked lips to Deena's ear. The stink of decay had now combined with her perfume, turning the comfort of White Shoulders into an assault.

Zahra whispered, "You recognize my perfume, yes? You remember *Odoratu*?"

Her whisper was joined by the dead souls of Deena's family, intoning an indictment, blaming her, accusing her. The chants of *Auditu* tumbled one over another like a monastery's mass for the dead.

"Stop!" cried Deena.

Her tears touched her lips, bringing the taste of *Gustu* to her tongue, first faint, then growing stronger, until the taste could barely be contained. It was the bitter taste of her callousness. The poisonous taste of her transgressions, forcing itself down her throat, where it entered into her ears and eyes and throat and skull. Deena saw clearly who she was and what she'd done.

She deserved to die.

With that thought, Zahra twisted and turned, changing shape and size until the *Sensu* in human form—Maggie's form—stood in front of her.

"Yes, Deena. You deserve to die. You caused immeasurable pain to someone who loved you unconditionally."

Deena sobbed, gulping in great mouthfuls of air. It was all true. The only thing left now was to put an end to it.

The *Sensu*/Maggie straddled Deena, lowering itself onto her lap until they were face-to-face. "Stay awake, my dear," it whispered, stroking her hair. "It is time."

Its fingers combed through Deena's scalp and traveled down the nape of her neck, bringing what Deena could only imagine was *Tactu*'s calling card. A clutter of spiders entered through her pores, skittering in and around every fold and crevice, traveling down her throat, into her chest, her stomach, between her legs, affecting every last part of her. But she knew, somehow, that this was just an appetizer. She stared at the *Sensu* as its eyes receded, replaced by someone else's.

Agatha's.

It was Agatha straddling her now, with a self-satisfied sneer. She brought her face in close, pried Deena's lips apart, and clamped her open mouth over Deena's.

Deena gagged at the feel of Agatha's dry lips sealed onto hers. Her aunt forced her breath into Deena's mouth and down her throat. And it didn't matter. It didn't matter.

Deena gave herself over as her aunt's thighs squeezed against her hips. Agatha then inhaled deeply, sucking the air out from Deena's lungs. Deena sighed.

And sighed.

And sighed again.

With each sigh Agatha absorbed another piece of her.

Deena tasted the anger on Agatha's breath. She saw the triumph in her eyes. She was being taken. She was being consumed. She was becoming . . . nothing.

When Agatha finally pulled away she grabbed Deena by the hair, roughly yanked her head back, and carefully examined her face.

Deena looked back at her aunt with her eyes glazed over and her jaw slack.

"I would say you're just about ready," said Agatha. She stood and pointed to the lake. "Look."

Deena tried to focus a few feet beyond where she sat.

The lake's surface was as smooth as polished onyx. And then it began to churn, as if the power lying in wait below the surface was too great to contain.

Agatha took a step behind Deena and grabbed her head with both hands, holding her eyelids open so that she had no choice but to watch. She brought her lips to Deena's ear and whispered, "*Tactu.*"

A vine as thick as a man's thigh broke through the surface dripping with thick, black sludge. It twisted in and around itself as it reached out toward Deena while Agatha stood behind the chair, keeping Deena in place. The closer the vine got, the tighter Agatha's grip became, until the vine wrapped itself around Deena's ankle.

Deena smelled her burning flesh before she felt the pain. But when it came, the pain was beyond anything she had ever experienced. It reached through her skin, past her muscles, to the bone, where it lodged itself into the very marrow. Then, using that bone as a conduit, the pain shot up through her leg, past her hips, and directly into her heart, where it grew so large, her chest threatened to burst from the heat of it. With each painful wave, tastes and smells and sounds and visions forced themselves into every corner of her being, growing so large and loud that she felt the boundaries of her body stretch to the point of breaking.

Deena let out an agonizing scream as the skin on her arms and legs reddened and then erupted into a field of pus-filled blisters. The pain was so great that the air in front of her eyes separated into floating objects going round and round her head.

She was close now. Nearly gone.

But then, through her half-closed eyes, Deena saw her mother glowing in the palest of yellows, floating toward her with a golden aura framing her face.

And this *was* her mother. The warmth of her smile and love in her eyes told Deena as much. But it was too late. Deena felt herself slipping away.

Agatha saw Zahra as well. She lunged at her mother's neck, but Zahra managed to swerve out of the way. Zahra wrapped her hands around Deena's right ankle and up her leg where the worst of the blisters had begun to burst. The feel of her mother's hands revived Deena just enough to reach out. She wanted to take her mother's hand one more time and let her know that she loved her. But when she looked down she saw the vine change direction and wrap itself around Zahra's waist.

Deena tried to warn her but it was too late. The vine tore her mother away, dragging her into the black lake. And just as in Deena's nightmare, Zahra looked back at her daughter with widened eyes, pleading, "Deena, help me."

Whatever weakness Deena had felt was suddenly gone. She forced herself up, ignoring the pain, and before Agatha could grab her, jumped into the lake.

The black bog coated her arms, legs, and neck as it tried to suck her down below the surface. Every part of her screamed to get out, but seeing her mother's sinking image pushed the thought away. She moved through the sludge and reached Zahra just as her mother was nearly immersed. With Zahra now in her arms, she headed to shore and somehow managed to push her up onto the bank.

Deena was just about to join her when the vine reared up and wrapped itself around Deena's neck, pulling her back into the lake. She gritted her teeth and flailed her arms in her effort to stay above the surface. Thank God she had at least gotten Zahra to safety. Deena looked back toward the shore in hopes that the sight of her mother would give her the strength to keep fighting.

But her mother *wasn't* safe. Agatha had grabbed hold of Zahra's legs and was dragging her back toward the lake. In a few seconds her mother would be right back where she'd started. It had all been for nothing.

And then, in Deena's peripheral vision the images of Simon, Fiona, and Kayla appeared at the water's edge, watching, with their faces calm and their mouths, slightly upturned. Deena looked from one to the other and remembered what Jadwiga had said: Her love for them would help her find the strength. She prayed that the old woman was right.

Deena grabbed the vine with both hands, locked her jaw, and with all her energy, focused on breaking free—but again, she failed. *What do I do?* she thought helplessly. She needed to get to her mother.

Deena looked back at the people she loved. "Help me!"

In answer to her call, they floated up off the bank and circled inches above her head, moving faster and faster until all Deena could see was a bright light shining above her. When the light was at its brightest, it cascaded over Deena and entered into her body. The warmth traveled down through her shoulders and into her arms. She felt Simon's strength and Kayla's goodness and Fiona's edge weave in and around who she was, turning Deena into the sum total of everyone she loved.

With their strengths a part of her now, Deena grabbed hold of the vine around her neck. The bright light of her loved ones shot out from every finger, growing thick and sinuous as they twisted around the vine. The bands of light then tightened their hold until the vine glowed white-hot from the fire that had been ignited deep within its core. The brighter the fire, the louder it roared, until, with one last great bellow, it disintegrated into a thousand burning embers, sputtering like fireflies on a summer night. They spread out over the surface of the lake and slowly sank.

Now free, Deena clawed her way through the mire until she reached the shore, and on hands and knees, pulled herself up onto the bank. Thick sludge was dripping off her body and blackening her face. She was just inches away from Agatha, who was bent over Zahra, pulling her closer toward the lake.

Deena grabbed her aunt by the shoulders, spun her around, and clamped her hand over her face. Agatha shrieked as Deena pushed her fingers deep into her eyes. Black liquid oozed from the sockets, reshaping itself into two horrific creatures—black serpents twisting in the air with their mouths stretched wide and their teeth bared, screeching. They circled Deena, looking for a way in, but Simon, Kayla, and Fiona formed a barrier of light blocking their entrance. They then focused their rage on Agatha, wrapping themselves around her neck and face. In a frenzied feeding they devoured the skin around the two black holes where her eyes had been, until her face became a single gaping wound. Her screams could not contain her suffering. A torrent of air engulfed her as she disintegrated into smoke with a final agonizing scream.

The lake receded and everything grew still.

Zahra reached her hand out to Deena as her lips formed a "Thank you." Then she faded away as Deena lay breathless on the shore.

35

Deena came to, collapsed on the cold linoleum floor in her aunt's room. Her burns were gone. When she pulled herself up, she discovered that everything was as it had been. Agatha lay in bed surrounded by monitors, with a chair sitting in the corner and an overbed table by its side. It was as if none of it had happened—except for Simon, crumpled on the floor, blood coming from a deep gash that ran from his forehead, across his left eye, and down the side of his face. His right leg was bent in a position that defied human anatomy.

"No!" Deena rushed over and knelt next to his unconscious body. He was alive, but only just. "I need help!" she yelled.

An orderly came in and saw Simon lying on the floor. "Oh my God! Hold on."

Two nurses came running. "What happened?"

"I—I'm not sure," said Deena. "When I walked in, this was how I found him."

The nurses called for help as they strapped on an oxygen mask and examined his wounds.

"It looks like a concussion. He's lost a lot of blood, and that leg will need to be set. We'll transport him to Hillcrest right away."

Deena kept her eyes focused on Simon as she stayed by his side. *He'll be all right,* she thought. *He has to be.*

They strapped him onto a gurney and Deena followed them out. But before she reached the hallway, a weak voice from the bed called her name.

"Deena," said Agatha, with her eyes searching. "I'm . . ."

Her aunt took in a quick breath and her eyes grew wide as she inched up off her pillow. A loud beep sounded from the heart monitor, bringing a doctor and two nurses rushing in. They surrounded Agatha and placed a defibrillator on her chest.

"Clear," the doctor called. There was a crack of electricity. And again, "Clear."

But no matter how great their efforts, they couldn't prevent the flat line on the monitor from proclaiming the news for all the world to hear—

Agatha Haddad, sister of Zahra Abdel, aunt of Deena Bartlett, killer of Nabil Abdel . . .

Agatha Haddad was dead.

36

TWO YEARS LATER

Deena walked into the dining room carrying an oversized platter of pasta.

"Damn," said Simon, plucking a sautéed mushroom off the platter. "Just how much food do you think we're going to need?"

"Kayla's friends are eating machines. I wouldn't be surprised if every falafel pushcart, hot dog stand, and juice bar within a five-mile radius of Tisch has run out of food."

"Deena, my love," yelled Fiona from the kitchen. "You need to come and see if this bread is ready to come out."

"Be there in a minute."

The doorbell rang. Simon adjusted the patch over his left eye and, with his cane, limped to the door. When he swung it open, Jadwiga smiled up at him from her wheelchair, with Oskar standing behind. He wheeled his grandmother in, not exactly smiling, but not exactly scowling, either.

"Now it's a party," said Simon, laughing.

He handed Oskar a beer and Deena brought Jadwiga a cup of tea while Fiona busied herself in the dining room, opening two bottles of wine.

Before long the door burst open and an invasion of four chattering theater majors rushed in. Deena shooed everyone into the dining room while she went back to the kitchen for the salad.

She walked down the hall flanked by framed photos on both sides. As she did, her eyes fell on a particular favorite: a fourteen-year-old Zahra getting drenched with a garden hose wielded by an even younger Agatha. The sight of the old picture brought to mind the terrifying upheaval from two years ago.

There were so many questions from that time that had been left unanswered. Deena would never understand why Agatha had hung on to her nineteen-year-old anger. And to this day, she had a difficult time reconciling that her parents had betrayed her aunt.

But overriding everything was Agatha's part in her father's death. There was a time when she wondered if her aunt had been trying to say *"I'm sorry,"* that night before she'd died, but that moment had passed. Apologies were never her aunt's style. Then again, who knows.

"Are you coming or not," yelled Simon from the dining room.

"Keep your shirt on."

Deena did a final toss of the salad and brought it into the dining room. Kayla and her friends were loudly one-upping each other with stories about their professors, while everyone else sat back and laughed—even Oskar.

Deena was lucky. She had a husband she loved. Jadwiga, who felt like a mother of sorts. Oskar, playing the part of the grumpy, depressed younger brother. Her lifelong friend Fiona. And of course, Kayla. Wonderful, talented Kayla. A younger version of herself, making her way toward an exciting life.

But every once in a while, when the house was quiet and she found herself alone, the images she'd been shown by the *Sensu* came back—all of them, fashioned from her past deeds. Deena would have to live with those images, always. Her one consolation was that she had seen the forgiveness in her mother's eyes. What's more, Deena had managed to save Zahra from whatever the *Sensu* had had in store for her. For now, that would have to be enough.

"All righty, then," said Deena, with an exaggerated flourish of her napkin. She cleared her throat, lifted her wineglass, and said, "Let's eat!"

———

Eight hundred miles away in an empty hospital waiting room, just outside Chicago, an exhausted John Philmont sat with his head in his hands, hoping for the best. The doctors had been working on his wife for hours, but there was no guarantee the heart surgery would be a success. After years of fighting, he never could have imagined feeling so at sea. Forty-three is too young to die. But it was as if all her anger, all her yelling, all the insults she'd hurled at him with expert marksmanship, had ricocheted back at her—a bull's-eye, straight to the heart.

John lifted his head at the sound of someone wheeling an IV stand down the hallway. It was a young boy, nine years old, maybe ten. He was cadaverously thin, with a bald head and deep circles under his eyes. And yet, he wore a smile. As he came closer, their eyes met and, with a wide grin, the boy said, "Wanna dance?"

ACKNOWLEDGEMENTS

I'd like to start by thanking my husband, Glenn who never once rolled his eyes when I said, "What do you think of this paragraph?" There is no more patient man on the planet. He is my partner, my confidant, my rock, and my love. He was one of my first readers and his comments on this book were pivotal. He also makes a great steak and tells a tremendous joke. How lucky am I.

Deena Undone would not have been written without the friendship, creativity, extraordinary sense of humor and artistic wisdom of Ken Bingham. It is true that his critique of every page was instrumental in whatever merit this novel may have. But more than that, Ken has the unique gift of gathering people from every persuasion and binding them together with joy and familial good cheer. His energy is infectious. His optimism is inspiring. And his friendship is one of my most prized possessions.

I would also like to acknowledge the two a.m. texts between Ken Bingham, Paolo Paciucci and myself that always manages to keep my creative juices flowing.

Along with Ken and Paolo is the extraordinary group of talented writers who read most if not all of this book and whose critiques contributed mightily to the final draft. Damn. There are so many! Robin Dondiego who was the book's first editor, Josephine Curry who read and commented on the entire novel, Thom, Sarah, Gretchen, Matt, Taden, Michael L., Michael D., Twinckle, David, Diane, JP, Mary, Patrick, Michele, Lynne (This is turning into a laundry list.)

To Steve Eisner, Alison McBain, Gregory Norris and cover designer, Asha Hossain, all from When Words Count. Thank you for your wisdom, support, and inspiration. This book wouldn't be happening if not for your guidance.

And speaking of When Words Count, I would never have met them if Linda Rappaport hadn't thrown my name and novel into the hat. I owe you so much, Linda.

To S.T. Joshi whose help and encouragement in the writing of this book made me feel as if I really was a writer. Thank you, also, for the over-the-top pre-publication blurb!

While I'm at it I would also like to thank Michael Aronovitz, Clay McLeod Chapman, Merideth Finn, and Bruce Makous for their blurbs. In addition, Michael has been a great supporter of my work. Coming from a horror writer with his experience, it means a lot.

A shoutout to the indomitable Gina Fox who was kind enough to go through my book with her fine-tooth comb.

To David LeGere and all the folks at Woodhall Press. I'm excited at the prospect of getting to know you. Thank you for helping me with this wacky publishing process.

To my boys, Matthew and Sam, who are never too shy to give their honest opinion.

And lastly, to my mother. I know you're watching. I wish you were here.

ABOUT THE AUTHOR

Debra K Every is a self-described adrenaline-seeking writer focused on horror, thrillers and stories that make the heart beat fast. In 2023 her first novel, *Deena Undone*, won gold at Pitch Week XXIX sponsored by When Words Count Retreat. Her short stories have appeared in *Unleash Creatives, Penumbra 2024 Annual, Querencia Press, Etched Onyx* and *Arzono 2023 Anthology*. Before turning her sights on writing, she spent years as a professional opera singer and finds herself using those same musical sensibilities in her current work.

Debra lives amongst the rolling hills and pastures of Upstate New York with her husband and quirky cattle dog, Bad Dog Bob, where they are regularly visited by a loud assortment of friends and their two grown sons.